Sweet Nothings

A Bethany Beach Romance

By Michael Geraghty

Published by Hold Fast Publishing

Hold Fast Publishing

1

Damian

I swiveled my leather desk chair around, so I looked out the window towards the blackness where I knew the Hudson River lay below. If I glanced left or right, I could see a hint of some of the city lights from the buildings around me, but I always chose to focus my attention more towards the water, even if I couldn't see it clearly. It was the water that had brought me to where I was today, first as a kid fascinated by the ocean, then as an inventor, and now as owner of STW Enterprises, the largest company focused solely on finding ways to preserve and save our oceans and waters. It was no fluke that I chose this office space, which during the daylight hours gave me a panoramic view of the Hudson like no other spot in the New York/New Jersey area.

"Damian, are you paying attention to any of this?"

The truth was, I wasn't paying attention to anything Paul Austin had to say. It wasn't that I disliked Paul; he worked hard, did his job well and had been the corporate head counsel for years now. It was just that what he usually told me was not very interesting, at least to me. It was probably something mundane, like a patent or copyright, a dispute with some company, some new land purchase, or a problem with some political connection that needed to be made either in the U.S. or some foreign country. They were all important, to be sure, but none of that was going to be enough to hold my interests right now.

I spun my chair back around to face Paul. He had the incredulous, bordering on being annoyed face he would often get with me, even if he would never say that's how he felt. I leaned back in my chair, letting it creak slowly because I knew it would make the hair on the back of his neck stand up. I could see his face cringe slightly with each cry out for WD-40. My guess is he would have maintenance in here at 5 AM tomorrow to make sure the chair got treatment.

"Paul, it's practically 10 PM. I know I've been here since 7, and you've probably been here just as long. I don't know that I could even tie my shoes right now, nevermind pay close attention to whatever you're trying to tell me."

"You're wearing loafers," Paul pointed out to me as he looked at my feet resting on the corner of my desk. I put my feet down on the floor and pushed myself out of my chair, and then walked towards the large windows that were behind my desk.

"I think you missed my point," I answered. "Don't you have a girlfriend waiting for you? It's Friday night. You should be out somewhere having dinner or going to a club instead of telling me about legal issues."

I stared out the window, but I could see Paul's reflection in the dark glass. He fidgeted in his chair before he decided to say something.

"My girlfriend broke up with me two weeks ago. She complained I worked too much. She sent me a text message to let me know. So, no, I don't have a girlfriend, but neither do you."
Paul sat back in his chair with a smug smile on his face.

"Once again, not the point, Paul," I said to him, prying my gaze away from the dim lights that were coming from some boats out on the water.

"So, what is your point then? That we both work too much? It's no secret, Damian, but it's because we do that this company has grown to the success it is and that thousands of people have jobs."

"The success of the company isn't going to change if we leave before 11 one night."

I reached over to my desk and closed my laptop and stuffed it into my well-worn brown leather bag. I then pressed the intercom button to talk to Shannon, my assistant.

"Shannon? You still here?" I spoke out.

"Still here," she said as papers shuffled in the background.

"Is everything all set?" Paul looked over at me as I spoke, wondering what was going on.

"Ready whenever you are," she answered. I could hear Shannon stifling a yawn. She was probably the hardest working person in this company.

"Great, thanks," I replied, and pressed the button off.

"Paul, I'm out of here," I said to him, grabbing my leather jacket off the back of my chair. "Whatever it is you have for me will have to wait a while."

"Okay, we'll talk about it in the morning," Paul told me as he stood up, straightening out his suit jacket and tie.

"I won't be here, and I'm not taking your call," I said as I started to walk towards my office door.

"Won't be here? Where are you going to be?" he asked in a panic.

"I'm taking some time off," I told him, opening my office door. I stepped out and could see Shannon gathering her things and turning off her computer.

"How long?" Paul said, grabbing his phone to check his calendar.

"I don't know. At least a week, maybe two. I bought a house and want to get it settled."

"You bought a house? What do you need a house for? You have a place in the city and places in Los Angeles and London. Who needs a house? And why am I just hearing about this? Shouldn't your lawyer get consulted on things like this?"

"I wanted a house on the beach, a place where I could go and relax and get away from all this," I said as I waved my arm around. "If I want to buy a house, I can do it; I don't need you to hold my hand through the process. I bought the place ten months ago, and they finally finished with renovations and furnishing the place, so now I want to see it. Why do I have to explain all this to you? Come on, Shannon, let's go."

I made my way through the maze of cubicles towards the elevator, while Shannon walked next to me. She took a quick peek back at Paul, who frantically tried to follow behind me.

"I think that vein in his forehead is bulging out," she said quietly as we walked out into the reception area.

I pressed the button for the elevator and sighed, turning back towards Paul. He was red-faced, and the vein was larger. If I looked close enough, it almost seemed like it was pulsing.

"Paul, relax." I put a hand on his shoulder. "Maybe you want to take some time off, too. Give yourself a chance to recharge your batteries. Take a trip, go on a cruise, go see your parents, do something. You need to get away from here before you completely burn out. That's what I'm doing."

"But... but what if something happens while you're gone, or while I'm gone?"

"That's why we hired all these other smart people around here. The business doesn't come to a grinding halt if you or I don't walk through the door."

The elevator door opened, and Shannon and I stepped inside. Paul went to follow us, but I put my hand up to stop him.

"Go back to your desk, get your stuff, and put a few days off on your calendar and do something else, anything else. Just don't call me. I'll see you when I get back."

The elevator doors slowly slid shut, and Paul's anxiety-ridden face disappeared behind them.

"You know he's going to call me all week instead," Shannon sighed.

"I know, and I'm sorry for that. Don't take his calls. This trip is just as much for you to relax as it is for me. You never take time off either, Shannon. Even when I'm off, you still work. Let's both try to make this an actual vacation for a change."

"I think I forgot how to do that," Shannon told me.

The elevator doors glided open to the parking garage. We were immediately greeted by James, my driver for the last five years. Standing there in his dark suit and tie, he smiled and nodded at me, and then at Shannon, taking the bags we had in our hands.

"James, did you get my luggage from the house?" I asked him as I opened the back door to the limousine.

"Picked them up this afternoon," he told me as he slammed the trunk shut.

"Shannon's bags too?" I asked him before he closed the back door to the limo.

"It's all taken care of Boss," James answered as he got into the front seat.

"Did you get your stuff as well?"

I could hear James exhale deeply as he looked back at me in the rearview mirror.

"Boss, I've been driving for you for a long time, on overnight trips and longer. Have I ever forgot to bring my bag?"

"No, James," I answered with a smile.

James raised the partition as he began to drive.

"How long is the ride to the house?" Shannon asked me as she reached into the small cooler in the back to grab a bottle of iced tea for herself and one for me.

"It's about five hours from here down to Bethany Beach," I told her as I loosened my tie so I could take it off. I already felt more relaxed than I had sitting in the office all day. I took a sip of the iced tea and leaned my head back against the headrest.

"Why don't you stretch out and get some sleep?" Shannon suggested as she shifted over to one of the side seats of the limo.

It was certainly tempting. I kicked off my loafers and laid down on the back seat, balling up my suit jacket to use as a pillow. I would probably regret doing that to my suit, but I didn't care so much; I just needed to get some relaxation going. I peeked over at Shannon and could see she had taken her heels off and was now sitting more comfortably on the seat, looking at her phone.

"I hope you're not working," I mumbled to her.

Shannon looked over at me with an arched eyebrow.

"No work. Just texting a friend to make sure they come over and water my plants for me while I'm gone. I'm going to listen to some music while you sleep, if that's okay, boss."

Shannon reached into her purse and pulled out a pair of black earbuds and plugged them into her phone.

"I'm not trying to be a dick, Shannon," I said to her. "I just want to leave the work behind for a bit. I would think you would appreciate that."

"I do appreciate it, and I'm looking forward to this, believe me. But we both know that when you say you are taking time off it usually doesn't work out that way. I'm never really on vacation you know. People always need something from you, which means they need something from me, or you need something from me."

I sat back up in my seat and looked at Shannon. She had started working for me right out of college, and I was impressed by her right away. I had gone through several assistants before she came along, and she has been the perfect combination for me of smarts, intuition, decision-making, and take-no-bullshit attitude. She did more to make sure this company runs well than I do, which is why she is one of the most well-compensated assistants out there.

"I promise, I'm going to try to keep that from happening this trip," I told her. "Maybe we can both have a good time for a change. The new house is great, the weather is supposed to be perfect, and you can just do whatever you want. Maybe you'll even meet someone while we're there."

"Me?" Shannon answered. "I'm the one that actually goes out on dates, remember? You're the person who stays home brooding in your penthouse apartment like Bruce Wayne. It's been months since you've gone out with anyone."

"I don't think it's been that long," I said defensively.

"Damian, I keep your calendar and schedule. Want me to look back and see?"

Right away, she typed in something on her phone, her thumb flying over the screen to flip back page after page.

"Here," she said emphatically, holding the screen up to my face. "February, you went to that charity dinner with that fashion model, Gabriella. That's six months ago."

I remembered Gabriella. She was an amazingly beautiful woman that I was set up with by a mutual friend. She was nice, but not much of a conversationalist. She spent most of the night chatting up the German race car driver that was seated next to her at our table. By the time that dinner was over, she was more interested in going home with him, and I was ready for her to leave.

"Yeah, that was kind of a bust," I said to Shannon. "Are you sure there hasn't been something else? I think I had gone to dinner with someone when that new restaurant opened in the lobby of our building last month."

Shannon just stared at me, knowing I was wrong.

"That was me, Damian. You said you didn't want to go through the hassle of finding a date and arm-twisted me into breaking a date I had that night so I could go with you."

I looked back at Shannon and realized she was right.

"Okay, so it's been kind of a dry spell for me, I admit it, but I like being by myself. I don't have to worry about trying to make conversation, or whether they are just out with me because I have money or so they can get their picture taken for some website."

"You can tell yourself that, Damian, to make yourself feel better, but we both know it's not true. No one wants to be alone all the time. Why else would you take James and me with you down to your house? You could have gone by yourself. Face it, you want companionship just as much as the rest of us."

Shannon sat back in her seat with a triumphant smile on her face.

So, I didn't date much. I knew it, and so did everyone around me, which is probably why people made such a big deal of it when I did go out somewhere with someone. Which was just another reason for me not to go on many dates. To be honest, I didn't count on or expect to do much of anything on this trip other than kick back, enjoy my home, and spend some time on the beach.

Shannon put her earbuds back in while I gazed out the window. We drove our way down the New Jersey Turnpike, and it wouldn't be too long until we reached the Delaware Memorial Bridge. From there, it was only a few hours more until we got down to the beach areas and the coast. If we were lucky, we would get to the house just about in time for sunrise, something I always looked forward to at the beach.

I was hoping this trip would bring me the mental and physical break I needed from work. Even if I did nothing for two weeks, it was worth it to me. If anything else came along during that time, it was fine, but I certainly wouldn't go looking for it. There would be no business, no stress, and no worries.

We drove past a pickup truck filled with beach gear and camping gear. Through the tint of the windows, I could make out a few college-age kids crammed into the truck, obviously heading down to the shore for some fun.

One of them yelled out the open window towards our car.

"Woo hoo! Party limo! Live it up, dudes!"

I just laughed to myself as we sped past the truck and put them behind us.

Oh yeah, living it up, I thought to myself. *I'm sure there will be plenty of that going on.*

2

Kelly

Try as I might, drowning out the chirping of my alarm at 4 AM never seemed to work well. The temptation to just roll over and go back to sleep was a great one, but I knew it's not something I could ever give into. It's not just that I needed to get up and go to work, but Alice, my trusty Golden Retriever, was so conditioned with me being up at 4 that she immediately wanted to go outside when she heard my alarm. If I didn't get up right away, it would be moments before she was scratching on the bedroom door to get out or jumping up on the bed so I could smell the hot morning pants that she loved to share with me. Morning breath of your own is bad enough, but the morning breath of a dog was enough to make sure you got up and started moving.

I sat up in bed, stretched and yawned, and my feet hit the cool wood floor of the bedroom before I quick-stepped over to the bathroom and got myself together for the day. It didn't take long for me to get ready anymore, especially since working in a bakery meant you didn't have to dress up or even always look your best if you worked in the kitchen all day. A quick shower, a brush of my teeth, and pulling my hair back into a ponytail is all I needed to do before I got dressed for the day.

After I let Alice run around in the backyard for a few minutes so she could do her business, I got her back inside, and she promptly parked herself in the bay window at the front of the house so she could watch the action outside while I was gone for the day.

"See you later, Alice," I told her, and gave her a kiss on her head before walking out the door.

It was already gearing up to be a sweltering day at the beach, which can be both good and bad for business. People came into the bakery all day long to take advantage of the cool air conditioning we offer, giving them a break from the hot sun right on the beach, but we got more people who wanted to use the bathroom instead of buying anything. It was days like this that made me glad that we closed by 3 PM.

I took a quick look at my car, an old 2003 Ford pick-up I have had for far too long but didn't want to give up and decided it was better to leave it at home today and take my scooter out of the garage instead. Parking down at the beach was hell on the weekends, and the scooter allowed me to get around better. I could tuck into a cool, small parking spot right near the bakery.

I pulled the scooter out and pushed my ponytail inside the helmet. The scooter jumped to life as I turned the key, and the headlight flickered on so I could get on my way to the bakery. The bakery on the boardwalk was a short walk from my house, not more than a mile or so, but by the time I was done for the day I was too tired, and it was usually much too hot for me to want to walk back home.

There was no traffic out and about early in the morning, other than the fishermen looking to get out to the beach as the sun came up to get their day started. I made a quick right turn up Pelican Drive and found my parking spot, tucked under the boardwalk and away from prying eyes. I opened the small storage area under the seat and pulled my lock out to secure things tightly. I've had scooters stolen twice over the years because I was lax or too trusting, and with so many people milling about our little town in the summer, there were too many nowadays that you couldn't seem to trust.

I took ten steps on the gravel and sand before I reached the staircase that led me up to the boardwalk and right behind the bakery. I unlocked the door and heard the familiar buzz of the alarm that let me know I was the first to arrive, as usual. I quickly shut off the alarm, flipped on the kitchen lights, and grabbed my apron to get things started for the day.

I tried to get as much prep work completed as I could before my sisters showed up to help with everything. When I opened Sand & Sprinkles four years ago, it was just my sister Jodie and me working the whole place. I did all the baking myself while Jodie worked the front and we struggled with everything for a while before we finally caught on with both the tourists and the locals. Once we were stable and successful, my youngest sister Alex starting working with us part-time, and then I was finally able to convince my mother to join in and work in the shop so Jodie could help me in the back.

I spent my time getting all the dough prepared and rested and then started using the dough we had prepped yesterday to get everything going. We learned along the way what sells well, what doesn't, and what locals want compared to what the tourists snatch up early in the morning. This time of year, we go heavier on the donuts, muffins, croissants, and pastries, and then we offer some dessert snacks like brownies and cookies. We also make sure to have coffee, tea, and bottles of water to keep everyone happy. I had lots of plans about how I would love to expand the place eventually, adding more seating, bigger cases, and the ability to do things like bagels and more of the cakes I love to make and decorate, but we just weren't there yet.

It wasn't long before Jodie wandered in, followed shortly by Alex and my mother. In the summer months, I usually hired one or two local teens to come in and help with the front, wait on customers, stock the cases, and clean, but they didn't get here until just before we opened at seven if they were reliable enough to get here on time. Finding good teenage help these days wasn't always easy, and the good ones were hard to keep around if you could only offer them minimum wage or a bit more.

"Good morning," I said as the group wandered in. Mom and Jodie smiled at me and said hello, while Alex gave a grunt and a scowl and walked out to the storefront to get the registers going and start getting the cases ready.

"What's wrong with her?" I asked as I cut sections of dough out at a rapid pace to use for our jelly donuts.

"She and Tyler had a fight last night," Mom said as she grabbed an apron. "Typical teenage romance stuff. I went through the same thing with both of you."

I looked over at Jodie and laughed.

"Both of us? You mean with Jodie. She was the one who always had all the boyfriends," I said, moving on from the jelly donut dough to let it proof.

"I can't help it if the boys liked me better, Kelly," she said as she bumped my hip with hers.

"Turn on some music," Jodie said to me, pointing to the speaker over on the shelf above my workstation.

I synced my phone up to the speaker and started to stream some music through, choosing something lively that would get us moving well this early in the morning. As Jodie and I began to dance around and sing as we worked, Mom just shook her

head and went out to the storefront, chasing Alex back into the kitchen with us.
"Alex, can you put the trays of turnovers in the oven?" I yelled over to her.

Alex picked up the trays one by one and slid them into the oven before finally slamming the door shut.

"Hey!" I scolded. "Careful with that! Don't take your anger with Tyler out on my equipment."

"Sorry," she said. Alex came over to where I was standing and started to cut out some of the cake donuts for me.

"What happened last night?" I asked. Jodie stopped her dancing and putting pastries together to listen as well.

"Tyler's a dick is what happened," Alex said as she slammed the donut cutter into a piece of dough, rattling the table.

"What did he do this time?" Jodie asked. Jodie took away the tray of donuts before Alex punched a hole through the tray.

"We were supposed to go out last night for dinner and then hang out at the beach. Instead, he calls me and says he and his buddies were going over by the end of the boardwalk to watch them move stuff into that big house they finished building. Really? You'd rather watch a bunch of guys moving furniture and equipment than be with me? I told him to go to hell and hung up on him. He never even bothered to try to call me or text me back. I am so done with him."

After Alex finished raging over Tyler, Jodie and I just looked at each other and smiled. Alex had been like this with her on-again, off-again boyfriend all through this year of school and

into the summer. We both figured within two days they would
be back together again.

"Someone's finally moving into that monster house, huh?"
Jodie said as she pushed a tray of pastries into another of the
ovens. "Whoever bought that place must be loaded."

"I heard it was some billionaire from New York," Mom said
as she walked into the kitchen, handing us each a cup of coffee
that she had just made.

"Edgar Wilson and his sons did some of the woodworking
inside the place. They say he spent almost nine million dollars
just to have the place built. It even has a swimming pool that
goes inside and outside."

I took a sip of my coffee and looked over at Mom.

"Who buys a house at the beach and gets a swimming pool?
He'll probably spend three days a year here, complain about
the town and everything in it, and then try to sell the place. It's
the same story with all these rich folks that come down here
thinking they own the town and are owed something because
they have lots of money. What a waste."

Mom, Jodie, and Alex all looked at me, surprised I had so much
to say about it.

"Wow, what got into you?" Jodie asked.

"I'm just tired of people like that coming in and disrupting our
town. I get they bring some money in with taxes and jobs to
build the house, but I hate their attitudes. You see it when they
come in here," I said waving my arm around. "They get all bent
out of shape because we don't have their half-caf soy latte with

sugar substitute, or the selection of donuts they want when they come in ten minutes before we close and complain that we are just small-town hicks. I can't wait for summer to be over sometimes."

"Summer brings in most of our customers though, Kelly, "Jodie answered. "We kind of have to put up with them if we want to stay in business. Besides, not every rich guy is going to be like Trevor Dawkins was."

"I told you, no one mentions his name around here," I answered curtly.

I knew Jodie was right, but I didn't have to like it. When the summer was over, our town went back to a beach town with about two thousand residents. During the summer, with the beaches filled and every hotel and beach house rented, they were tens of thousands of people in the area for months. While most of the customers that came in were nice and friendly, I still had a chip on my shoulder about the others who felt they were entitled to everything and the kitchen sink and at as low a price as possible.

"Angela told me Derek was there last night with Tyler and the other guys," Alex chimed in. "Derek said they were bringing in all kinds of expensive looking stuff. It looks like whoever it is plans on doing a lot of entertaining."

"Man, I would love to get a look inside that place," Jodie said.

"They have their own gated entrance and private beach access. The town closed off Neptune Path and gave it to the owner. Everyone has to go a block down now if they want to get to the beach," Mom told us.

"See!" I yelled. "That's what I mean. Why is it okay for everyone else to be inconvenienced so some rich guy can sit out on his patio without seeing anyone else? It's not fair."

I blew a strand of hair that was on my face in a huff and wiped my floured hands on my apron. I looked over and watched Jodie take some items out of one of the ovens to cool. The warm smell of cinnamon raced through the air as the oven door opened.

"Hey, Jodie," I said to her. "I have an idea. How about you make up one of your gift baskets with some of our stuff, and we bring it over to that house after work today? Then we can see the house and just how pretentious the owner is and what they are all about."

"Wow, you really have your panties in a twist over this house," Jodie said to me. "Sure, I can make something up. I'll put a few things aside as the day goes along to put in there and make it look pretty, a nice welcome to the neighborhood basket. But what if they don't even let us in the gate?"

"If they don't, then we'll know what a jerk the guy is and let everyone in town know it, too," I said with a smug smile.

I went back to work with relish, working on some more dough and looking forward to proving myself right about our new, wealthy neighbor.

3

Damian

By the time we arrived in Bethany Beach, it was 5 AM, and the town was quiet. There were signs of the sun getting ready to rise, and you could see some of the early morning joggers and fishermen making their way out towards the beach and the boardwalk to start their day before it got too hot out there. Riding through town in a limo at 5 AM turned the few heads that were out and about, and I am sure people were wondering just who we were and where we were going.

Shannon had been sound asleep for hours, curled up on the bench seat opposite me. I had put a blanket on her so that she wouldn't get too cold from the frosty chill of the air conditioning in the car. I had tried to get some sleep, but I have always had trouble sleeping in the car and just couldn't get comfortable. Besides, my mind raced with thoughts about the business, the new house, and a thousand other things. Even though I had sworn to make this trip a relaxing one, following through on that might prove to be more difficult than I wanted to believe.

I started to feel anxious the closer and closer we got to where I knew the house was. I had come down to the site several times over the months since I bought the property and was having the house built, but I had yet to see the finished product with all the furnishings and everything inside. I had left the design work up to the interior design company I had hired, and they had spent many hours with me going over every painstaking detail of each room to make sure everything was just how I wanted it. To be honest, a lot of that stuff I cared very little about, like the color of the throw pillows on the couch, what plates were available in the kitchen and minute things like that. There were some extras I had insisted on that I wanted to make sure were there that may have seemed a bit outrageous to some people but would make it into the home I always wanted to have for myself.

I had several apartments in different parts of the country that I could stay at when I wanted to, but none of them ever really seemed like a home to me. They were just places I would visit, much like the different hotel rooms I stayed at when I traveled. The place in New York probably came closest to feeling like a home, but even then, I spent so much time working that it just became a place for me to catch a few hours of sleep before going back to work. I never entertained anyone there, had friends over to watch a game or brought a date there.

This house would be my home, the space that was truly mine to do what I wanted when I wanted. The location worked well since it wasn't too far from the New York office or from Washington, where I did a lot of business with the government. Sure it would be busy with tourists during the summer months, but for the rest of the year, it would be a quieter place where I could enjoy life without the pressures that usually surrounded me.

We finally pulled down the private road where the house was located, slowly making our way closer to the front gate. I could hear the tires crunching over the sand and shells and lowered the partition that James had put up between himself and us so that we could sleep while he listened to music on the ride down. A wrought iron gate surrounded on both sides by carved beige stone walls marked the driveway. The car came to a stop by the gate, and James then pressed a button on the remote he had in the car to swing the gates open. The limo slowly made its way down towards the house, coming to a stop just under the carport near the front of the house but not quite to the garage area.

"Here we are," James announced as he put the car in park and shut it off. I took off my seatbelt and reached over to give Shannon a gentle nudge to wake her. Her eyes slowly fluttered open as she gazed up at me.

"Good morning, sunshine," I said to her with a smile.

"Are we finally here?" Shannon asked grumpily as she wiped the sleep from her eyes and sat up.

"Try not to sound too excited about it," I answered her as I opened the car door, anxious to get out and stretch my legs.

As soon as I stepped out of the car, I was hit by the heavy warmth of the air and the wonderful smell of the ocean. I heard the waves crashing out towards the back of the house, bringing a smile to my face.

Shannon finally climbed out of the car and her face twisted up right away.

"Oh god, it's hot here. Let's get inside to the air conditioning," she said as she rushed past me to the front door.

I looked over at James, who just shrugged as he grabbed some bags out of the trunk.

"Damian, come on," Shannon yelled back to me. She stood by the front door, frantically turning the door handle to open the door.

"What is your rush?" I said as I walked up the steps to reach the front door.

"I'm hot, I'm tired, I'm cranky, and I have to pee," she said to me. "Where's the key?"

"It uses a passcode," I replied. I took out my smartphone, opened the app that had the door code built into it, and held it up to the sensor for the door.

"Are you kidding me with this stuff?" she said in a huff.

"It's more secure," I said as we heard the door unlock. Shannon quickly turned the handle and rushed inside, only to hear the beeping of the alarm system.

"Now what?"

"It's the house alarm. Hold on, I'll shut it off," I said, walking over to the alarm pad.

"Screw it," she said to me as she kept walking down the hall. "I can't wait anymore. If the police show up, you can explain to them I couldn't hold it any longer."

Shannon turned into the bathroom and slammed the door shut as I turned off the alarm. I switched on the hall lights in the downstairs portion of the house.

James had walked up behind me carrying a couple of the bags.

"I guess she's a little grouchy," James said as he came inside.

"Just a bit," I answered. "James, your room is down the hall, on the end to the left. Shannon's is the room just before yours. The game room is down here with its own bar and small kitchen, and there's a laundry room down here as well. I'm going to head upstairs and look around a bit to see how everything is."

"Where do you want your bags?" James asked me.

"You could just toss them on the elevator and send them up to the first floor. My room is up there."

"Whatever you say, boss. After I get the bags in, I am going to crash for a few hours. When I wake up, I think I'll wash the car off," James said as he started walking down the hall.

"James," I yelled at him. "Don't rush to do that. This is your time off too. Sleep as long as you want and relax."

"We'll see," he said as he dropped two bags in front of Shannon's door and then walked down to his, going inside the room.

I knew James wouldn't do as I asked. When I hired him years back, I hired him to be more than just a driver. James is a driver/bodyguard/friend, and he took each role he has in my life seriously. He had a military background that came in handy on more than one occasion, and his driving skills are second to none, whether he is driving the limo, a sports car, or a Jeep. James kept himself in impeccable shape, something that caught the eyes of the ladies no matter where we happened to go or whatever he happened to wear. He's been my constant companion on every trip I have taken for five years. Even though there may not be much of a call to have a bodyguard in my mind, the board of directors started insisting on it when I would get threats from different fanatics on one side or another. Also, when you have money, people tend to come out of the woodwork and try and say crazy things, so having James around gave me peace of mind. More than once I had seen him wrestle someone to the ground or move me through a crowd with lightning precision.

I slowly made my way up the stairs, stopping on the second floor just to take a quick look around. There were four more bedrooms located on this floor, along with the workout rooms and access to the special swimming pool I had asked for. The pool looked great and was massive, having an indoor portion that led directly to an outdoor portion into the backyard that was closest to the ocean. The pool used ocean water, filtering it to clean it up, and it was a sparkling clear color both inside and out. There was plenty of room around the pool deck in both locations for deck chairs, and there were umbrella tables available outside, along with a couple of cabanas. The inside area of the pool also had a hot tub for use.

I walked to the top floor, where there was an immense living room space, dining room area, and kitchen, along with my master bedroom. There were also decks on both sides so that you could sit out on the side facing the ocean, over the pool area, or on the front side of the house. My bedroom had access to either deck so I could choose what I wanted to do. I was impressed by the job the design team had done with all the furniture, and everything looked comfortable and homey, just the way I wanted it.

I entered my bedroom, with its king-size bed against the far wall, a couple of sitting chairs, and a TV and sound system all set up already. There was also a large walk-in closet that was already filled with some of the clothing I had sent ahead of my arrival, so I didn't have to worry about packing or traveling with a lot of things right away. I opened the curtains covering the glass windows and doors that led out to the wood deck on the ocean side and stepped outside. The warm ocean breeze caught me right away, and the taste of salt was in the air and in my mouth already. With the sun rising now there was a brilliant color lighting up over the ocean as I watched the waves roll gently in and out. I sat myself down in one of the high, white wooden deck seats so I could just watch, listen and enjoy.

The silence was broken quickly as I saw Shannon open one of the glass doors leading from the living room and walk out onto the deck. She strode over to me and leaned against the railing, looking out towards the beach access and the ocean.

"Pretty amazing, huh?" I asked her as I kept watching the ocean.

"It is beautiful, Damian, I'll give you that," Shannon said. She turned back to me, and then walked over and sat in one of the chairs next to me.

"How's your room?" I said.

"It's incredible," she said to me with a smile. "I think it's nicer than my bedroom in my apartment. You really didn't have to go that much trouble."

"I wanted you to be comfortable here. That's your space here whenever you want to use it. James' room is the same. You two are important to me, and I want to make sure that you have what you need and can enjoy your time here."

"Well, I think I am going to enjoy my time here by going down and getting some good sleep if that's okay," Shannon said as she stood up from the chair. She yawned widely, and I could see that she needed some rest.

"Go to sleep. I am going to stay up for a while. I think I am going to go for a run before it gets too hot. It will give me a chance to see some more of the area."

"You're crazy," Shannon replied. "You're supposed to be on vacation, and you're going to go for a run in the heat? Have fun with that."

Shannon gave me a light wave and went back inside. I took one more look out onto the ocean, watching the seagulls dive back and forth over the water, getting a morning snack. I could see off in the distance a couple of dolphins jumping in the water.

This place is perfect, I thought as I wandered back into my bedroom.

I stripped out of yesterday's suit that I was still wearing and found a pair of running shorts and a compression shirt to put on for my run. After grabbing a pair of my favorite running shoes from the closet and putting them on, I was ready to head out the door. I made sure to remember to grab the fob that would let me back in the front gate after I went out, and then made my way down the stairs and out towards the front door. Shannon and James must have both been in their rooms sound asleep because the place was completely quiet when I left.

I decided to run right on the beach to start out with, placing myself close to the edge of the water where the sand was firmer and easier to run on. I glanced out over the water as I moved along to see the sun dance along the wave tips. I spotted a few people heading out to try to catch some early morning waves for surfing, and there were other runners along the beach that passed me as I went, barely looking over at me as I went by. There was also a fair share of couples walking along the beach, young and old, holding hands or just walking together. I thought about how nice it would be to have someone I could share all this with, stroll on the beach with, and hoped that someday I could have the same smile on my face as each person seemed to have that I came across.

After heading down the beach for quite a while and then making my way back towards the house, I decided for my first run here I wanted to see a bit more of the boardwalk area. I hadn't spent a lot of time in this area since I was a kid and my parents would come down this way for vacations now and then. My father was a long-time congressman from New York and we would occasionally vacation here when he would get a recess in the summer. My mother always loved to come to the beach more than he did, and my brothers and I would spend all our time in the water, on the sand, or wandering the boardwalk looking for things to do.

As I got to the beach by my house, I turned left and headed up towards the boardwalk. The house was just off the end of the boardwalk itself and was separated just by the walls we had erected to surround the house and backyard area. Once I was up on the boardwalk, I started my run at a slow pace, just taking in the area and seeing what was around. It was still early, just after seven, but people were already out and about, staking claim to their positions on the beach or wandering up and down the boardwalk. Most of the shops wouldn't open for a while, but there were a few breakfast spots that people were going in and out of to get their morning coffee or breakfast sandwich.

I made my way further down the boardwalk, feeling the planks hard beneath my feet. The boardwalk itself wasn't quite half a mile long, so I figured I would turn around at the end, go back towards the house, and then do it again once more to finish off my run in my first time out. By the time I made my second pass, the sun was getting warmer, and I had worked up a bit of a sweat. I had gotten so accustomed to running on a treadmill at home or the gym that I could feel the difference in my feet and legs from pounding on the boardwalk. I had gone about three-quarters of the way back to the house when I decided to slow down to a walk for the rest of the way.

As I strolled along, I came across a quaint spot I was not familiar with. I looked up and saw the pastel-colored sign that read 'Sand and Sprinkles.' I looked through the window and could see there was a bit of crowd in the place, with people loading up on pastries and donuts. I pulled the glass door open and was hit with a cold blast of air conditioning as soon as I opened the door, fogging up the sunglasses I was wearing so I had to take them off. I could feel goosebumps forming on my arms and legs, and a chill raced up my back as I got on line to order.

The shop was well kept, clean, and beautiful inside. Just the smells in the air from all the baking were enough to bring a smile to your face. There were a few tables scattered against the far wall with patrons sitting, enjoying a coffee and a treat before starting their day. People ahead of me were getting bags of donuts, muffins, pastries, and cookies. I craned my neck around the long line to try to get a better look at what was in the display cases.

I scanned over to one of the cases and saw that they still had a good assortment of donuts, including jelly donuts that were covered either in powdered sugar or granulated sugar. I could remember eating donuts like this when I was a kid, with my grandfather going down to the local bakery to get us donuts and hard rolls every Sunday for us to enjoy for breakfast. It had been many years since I had indulged in a donut like this, and I knew I had to try one to see how it was.

I had just gotten up close to the counter, with two other people ahead of me still waiting for their orders. The two women behind the counter, one older and one much younger and both with the same red hair, were hastily packing treats into bakery boxes and tying them off. The older woman glanced at the line forming behind me and yelled out.

"Kelly! Can you help at the counter?"

Within seconds, a woman appeared from behind the swinging doors which I assumed led into the kitchen. She walked over to the register at the counter in front of where I was standing. I could see her apron dotted with signs of baking, and she had a hint of flour dusting the front of her blond hair. She looked up at me with a bright smile and brushed away the single strand of hair that had fallen in front of her dark brown eyes.

"Hi there," she said to me. "What can I get for you?"

I found myself staring at her longer than I probably should have, and the older gentleman standing in line behind me gave a light cough and gentle push of my shoulder, getting my attention and pointing at the counter so I could place my order and keep the line moving.

"Oh... I'm sorry," I said, feeling flustered. The woman just grinned wider at me.

"I'd like one of the sugared jelly donuts, please," I asked her, pointing to the donuts with the granulated sugar.

"Coming up," she said to me. I watched her pull on a pair of plastic gloves and grab a piece of tissue paper before gently plucking a donut off the pile and placing it in a small, white paper bag. She rolled the top of the bag down and placed it on the counter in front of me.

"Anything else?" she asked me.

"That's it," I told her.

"That's one dollar," she asked as she punched the transaction into her register. I reached down for my pocket to get my wallet and quickly realized that not only was my pocket not there since I was wearing running shorts, but my wallet was nowhere to be found either. I had left it back in my bedroom on my bureau when I was getting changed and had nothing on me right now.
I could feel my face turning red as I patted the sides of my shorts. I looked over at the woman waiting on me and tried to crack a smile.

"This… this is embarrassing," I said to her. "I don't have my wallet on me, I'm sorry."

The man behind me let out a frustrated sigh, clearly loud enough so I would hear him and feel that much smaller now.

"Thanks anyway," I said to her, and I pushed the bag back towards her. I'm sure the disappointment showed on my face, along with my embarrassment. I started to turn to walk away.

"Wait," the woman called out to me. She held out the bag with the donut in it, waiting for me to take it.

"Take it, please, it's fine," she said to me. "Having a donut will make your day better, trust me. Enjoy it."

"Thank you so much," I said to her, grasping the bag in my hand. Our hands touched briefly as I smiled at her again.

"I promise I'll be back to reimburse you," I said honestly.

"No need," she said to me. "Just tell people you had a great donut and service here, and pay it forward, okay?"

"You bet," I replied, holding up the bag. I moved out of the way and could hear the man behind me mutter "Finally," as he stepped forward to the counter.

I looked back as I was walking towards the door and my eyes met hers again. I bumped right into someone coming through the door, causing them to drop the bag they were carrying and bringing some giggles from other patrons and from the nice woman who waited on me.

I finally got out of the bakery and stood outside by the front window and opened the bag. I held the bag up to my face and just breathed in the smell of the donut. I inhaled the familiar smell of the yeast and the sugar and was brought right back to my childhood. I eased the donut out of the bag and took a bite, savoring the flavor and the raspberry jelly inside as it hit my tongue. Naturally, a gob of jelly also oozed out down onto my shirt, but I didn't even care about it. I devoured the donut in no time at all, wiping the sticky trail of sugar from my lips and then the jelly that was inching its way down my shirt, leaving smudge marks to mix with the sweat that had formed.

I was almost tempted to go back in and get a bottle of water or a cup of coffee before I remembered I had no money on me. The thought crossed my mind just to go back in and tell that woman how wonderful the donut was and how nice she was for giving it to me, but as I peered through the window, I could see she was no longer at the counter.

I stepped back just as the grumpy patron who was behind me was coming out of the bakery, bumping into him once again and jostling the cup of coffee he had in his hand.

"Buddy, you need to get your head in the game today," he said to me gruffly as he held the coffee away from his body, so it didn't spill on him. He moved off to the side and started making his way down the boardwalk in the opposite direction I needed to go.

I walked the rest of the way back to the house, still tasting the donut in my mouth, and feeling satisfied from the run. I reached down into my sock and pulled out the remote to activate the gate so it would open and made my way inside and down the driveway toward the house. After punching in the code, I stepped inside and felt the air conditioning flowing nicely in the house. I was sure Shannon had turned it up to make things even cooler while she slept.

I walked up the stairs, deciding to forgo jumping in the pool to cool off, and instead went up to the bedroom to shower and change. I walked into the bedroom and saw my suit jacket laid out on the bed, and my wallet resting nicely on top of the bureau, along with my watch.

I peeled of the sweaty and sticky shirt I had on and tossed it into the wicker hamper in the corner of the room. That jelly stain on the shirt would be a bitch to get out.

All worth it, I thought to myself with a smile.

I knew I would be returning to the bakery, and not just to pay them back for the donut.

4

Kelly

With the warm weather outside, there was a constant flow of business into the bakery from the time we opened the doors at seven until we finally shut the doors at three. All of us were exhausted, but as is the case with a business like this, we spent another hour or two cleaning everything up and doing prep work for tomorrow to make the morning go smoothly. Getting dough started for morning buns and sticky buns, prepping donut dough, restocking supplies so they are at hand easily, and other chores like this are all part of our routine. It doesn't matter how tired you may feel after the day – all this stuff needs to be done so the next day goes well.

As we wrapped everything up, and Mom closed out the registers and put the cash in the safe, I saw Jodie putting the finishing touches on the basket she was making to bring to the big beach house. She had crammed it full of pastries, cookies, and brownies. She tied some nice blue ribbon on it, and even put one of our coffee mugs with some ground coffee in the bag as well.

"Looks great, Jodie," I said to her, admiring her work.

"I think it will do the job," she said.

We both took off our aprons and placed them on one of the workstations. Mom quickly snatched them up and stuffed them into her bag.

"I'm doing laundry tonight, so I'll wash everything," Mom said as she grabbed some of the towels lying around as well. "Are you two coming for dinner?" she then asked.

We both looked at each other, knowing neither one of us had anything else to do tonight.

"I guess I'll be there," Jodie said to Mom.

"How about you, Kelly?" Mom said, waiting patiently for an answer.

"She doesn't have anything better to do, Mom. She'll be there," Jodie stated for me.

"Okay, dinner is at six. I'll see you two later." Mom looked around the kitchen to make sure everything looked okay. "Alex, I'm ready to go," Mom yelled.

Alex popped in from the storefront and came into the kitchen.

"I'm going to meet Amber and Rhiannon down at the beach, if that's okay?" Alex asked.

"That's fine," Mom told her, seeming skeptical about what would happen. "Just be home by six for dinner."

"That's only an hour from now," Alex whined. "I can get something to eat down here. Please, Mom."

"No, you can be home for dinner at six. We have to work tomorrow," Mom reminded.

Mom gave us a smile and walked out the back door. As soon as the back door had closed, Alex let out a sigh.

"I'm glad she let me go," Alex said as she stripped out of her t-shirt and jeans, revealing the paisley bikini she was wearing. She slid into a pair of flips and looked at Jodie and me.

"Does Mom know you're wearing that?" Jodie asked her.

"No, that's why I waited until she left. And you're not going to tell her either," Alex said to Jodie. "I just bought this yesterday. It's so cute."

Jodie and I looked at each other, stunned.

"Alex," I said to her, trying not to sound too much like the big sister, "You're practically falling out of that thing it's so small."

"Relax, Kelly," she told me, adjusting the top of her bikini to push her cleavage out even more. "You know, if you two would actually wear something a little sexier to the beach instead of those old lady one-piece suits, you might actually have boyfriends." Alex smirked as she put her t-shirt on over her barely-there bathing suit.

"Get out you brat!" Jodie yelled, snapping a towel at Alex and catching her on the behind. Alex laughed as she went out the back door.

Jodie went back over and picked up the basket and carried it to the back door. I grabbed my backpack and put it on my back, set the store alarm, and we both went outside.

As hot as the kitchen can get while we are baking, it seemed even hotter outside today. The bright sun made me squint as soon as we walked out the door, and I stopped and reached for my sunglasses and put them on so I could be more comfortable. Jodie and I ambled along the boardwalk, heading towards the edge where the large house was located.

"Do you think Alex is right?" Jodie asked me as we walked through the crowd on the boardwalk.

"About what?" I said as I sidestepped a couple of seagulls munching on someone's lost French fries.

"About dressing sexier," Jodie said. Realizing she had said that louder than she intended and had gotten some looks from guys around her, Jodie smiled and laughed.

"Jodie, come on. She's eighteen, she doesn't know anything about dating, relationships, or guys beyond high school."

"I know," Jodie answered, "but she is the one with a boyfriend. I don't know about you, but it's been it's been about a month since I even went out on a date."

"A month? That's no big deal," I answered. I knew it had been much longer for me, and I was hoping Jodie wouldn't bring it up.

"All I'm saying is maybe we need to make more of an effort to put ourselves out there."

Jodie and I had reached the end of the boardwalk and could see the high wall that surrounded the property now.

"Put ourselves out there? You mean like Alex who was bursting out of her bikini? No thanks, I don't need attention like that," I answered as we turned and made our way down the staircase.

"That's not what I meant, Kelly, and you know it. I mean we should go out more, have some fun, maybe meet some new people, some men."

We turned and starting walking down the road towards the large iron gate.

"Jodie, I work six days a week and so do you. I don't know that I have time to go out and meet people, never mind start a relationship. I'm just trying to keep our business going."

We stood in front of the big iron fence, trying to figure out what to do next. There was a buzzer located on the wall to my left, and I started to walk over to press it. Before I could get there, I noticed Jodie had stopped in her tracks and was staring at something inside the gate. I walked over to her and tapped her on the shoulder.

"What's going on?" I asked her.

Jodie just pointed with her left her hand, and I followed her gaze. I immediately saw what she was looking at. There was a man there without his shirt on, washing the black limousine in the driveway. He was reaching over the hood of the car, scrubbing it down with a large sponge. You could see that he had a finely-toned body as the muscles on his back worked as he moved on the car. You could see the marks of tattoos on his left shoulder and his right bicep.

"That's what I'm talking about, Kelly," Jodie whispered as she kept her eyes locked on him. "I think I got pregnant just watching him wash the car."

"Yes, he's very attractive," I said to Jodie. "But we have a job to do here."

"You're right," Jodie said as she approached the gate.

"Excuse me!" she yelled, getting the attention of the man.

He turned to face us and smiled, and then tossed the sponge into the bucket beside him. He slowly walked over towards the gate, and we could see even more definition in his six-pack abs and pecs.

"What can I help you ladies with today?" he said to us.

There was a mixture of sweat glistening on his forehead and water dripping down his body seductively. The image was like it was right off the cover of a romance novel. The top of his shaved head was a bit red from the sun.

Jodie was immediately tongue-tied and couldn't say anything, so I stepped forward.

"Hi, I'm Kelly Barton, and this is my sister Jodie. I own Sand and Sprinkles, the bakery here on the boardwalk. We just thought we would stop by and give you this basket to welcome you to the neighborhood. It's quite a house you have here."

The man walked over and pressed the button on his side of the gate, and the gate retracted into the walls. Jodie and I stepped across, and I gave Jodie a nudge so she could break the spell she was in for the moment and hand him the basket.

"Well thanks, that's very kind of you," the man said to us, taking the basket. "But I'm not the owner of the house. I'm James, James Colbert. Mr. Woods is the owner of the house. I'm his driver and bodyguard."

"Bodyguard, hmmm," Jodie said with a smile. I could tell it was taking all her strength not to reach over and touch James' body.

"Is Mr. Woods available? We would love to meet him and say hello," I asked, still hoping to go inside the house and see the kind of gaudiness the house was decorated with. I imagined Mr. Woods as some overweight, entitled, rich man with too much money and time on his hands that wouldn't even say thanks for the basket.

"I can check, hold on one second," James said. He reached into his pocket and picked up his cell phone. He pressed a button and started talking into the phone.

"There's a couple of people from one of the local businesses here. They have a gift for Mr. Woods and want to know if they could bring it to him."

We waited patiently for an answer as Jodie kept looking up and down over James' body. I think he started to feel self-conscious about not wearing a shirt and reached over into the limo and grabbed his t-shirt and pulled it on. The t-shirt clung closely to his body, and Jodie reached her hand over to mine and squeezed it tightly.

James simply said, "Thanks," into the phone and hung it up.

"Sorry ladies," James said apologetically. "We didn't get down here until about 5 AM or so, so we were all pretty tired. Mr. Woods is asleep now."

"The drive didn't seem to wear you out any," Jodie said with a sly smile.

James laughed at Jodie's comment.

"I have the easy job," James answered. "He's the one running the billion-dollar company."

"Oh," I said to James. "We were wondering if it was some famous actor or rock star that moved in."

"Sorry to disappoint you," James said, looking over at Jodie, still staring at him. "Mr. Woods founded and owns STW Enterprises."

"I never heard of them," Jodie said. She acted like a giddy schoolgirl now, her left foot scraping along the driveway back and forth.

"Yes, you have, Jodie," I said, trying to snap her back to reality. "They're the company that makes all those things that are designed to help preserve and save the oceans."

"That's right," James said to me. "They do a lot of great work, and he's a good man to work for."

"Well, I guess we'll let you get back to work James. It was nice to meet you and thanks for passing the basket along. I hope you get to enjoy some of the snacks in there," I told him as I shook his hand.

Jodie thrust her hand out quickly to shake James' hand as well, and placed her left hand on his arm, feeling the muscles he had before slowly breaking away from him.

"It was nice to meet both of you as well," James said. "I'll bring this inside now and let Mr. Woods know you came by. I am sure he will stop by the bakery to say thanks."

"Great, thank you, James," I told him.

"Yes, thank YOU, James," Jodie said breathlessly.

I reached over and grabbed her hand and tugged her along behind me until we were back outside the gate. James reached over and pressed the button to close the gate behind us, and we watched him disappear into the house with the basket.
"Well that stinks," I said to Jodie as we made our way back up to the boardwalk.

"What stinks? That was awesome!" Jodie said. "Did you see the muscles on that guy? When he put that t-shirt on, I just wanted to go over and rip it right off him."

"That's not what I am talking about Jodie," I told her. "And you're right by the way; you obviously need a night out somewhere. You couldn't have acted hornier. I meant we didn't get to see inside the house or meet Mr. Woods. I would have liked to have met him, acted all nice, and then let him know what I think of him and his giant house taking up all that space and closing off the beach access there."

"You said his company does good things to save the ocean," Jodie told me. "And James said he's a good guy to work for. Maybe he's not the jerk you think he is."

"Of course James is going to say that, he gets a paycheck from the guy," I shot back. "Maybe his company does good things just so he can make a lot of money and he is a jerk personally. I've been around these rich guys plenty when I went to culinary school, Jodie. They all think that their money entitles them to whatever they want. They may put on a public display, but behind the scenes, they can be assholes."

We walked back to where the bakery was and down the steps to my scooter.

"You need a ride to Mom's?" I asked Jodie.

"I'm not getting on that thing with you," Jodie said, backing away. "You drive that like a maniac. I'll take my car over, thanks. Besides, the walk to my car will give me a chance to think more about James washing that limo."
"Whatever you say," I said with a laugh.

I unlocked my scooter, strapped my helmet on, and started up the scooter to head off. I worked my way over to Neptune Path and came to a stop on the scooter, so I could have a look down at the house. Plenty of people were walking along the street to catch a glimpse of the place before moving on to the next block so they could get beach access.

I sped off towards my Mom's house, kicking up some gravel and sand from the street as I left.

I should have given him some of the day old, stale muffins, I thought to myself, trying not to get angrier about what Mr. Woods would be doing in his mansion on the beach tonight.

5

Damian

I spent the bulk of the rest of the morning and afternoon getting my room in order, putting clothing away and trying to get my office organized with what I might need. I then browsed through the kitchen, seeing how it was stocked with food, supplies and the like in case I wanted to do any cooking. I hadn't done much cooking of my own in years, even though I loved to do it. There just wasn't enough time to do it myself, and I found myself going out more or ordering in. When I bought the house, the realtor gave me the names of some private chefs in the area if I ever needed anyone, but that felt too decadent to do.

After my housecleaning, I went and explored the rest of the house. The top floor had the full kitchen, my bedroom, a dining room, a living room with a bar area, sun porches, and bathroom. Down on the second floor was the pool, the exercise rooms, which I had them outfit with all the equipment I would like, including some of the boxing equipment and a ring to work out in. Boxing had become my exercise of choice over the last couple of years. It had been a great way to get out stress and aggravation that business, politics, and my personal life could provide, and I didn't want to miss out on it if I could avoid it. The second floor also had four more bedrooms, each with its own bathroom, and a small sitting area.

The bottom floor I had reserved primarily for Shannon and James, and they had the only bedrooms down there. I made sure each room was built so they would be most comfortable, getting input from them and using what I knew about them, so they had everything they needed. The game room was also down on the third floor, with a bar area, big screen TV, pool table, jukebox, and sitting room. There was even a separate room down there that was a small movie theater with a movie screen that we could use.

The house looked perfect, and the builders, designers and everyone involved had done a great job putting it all together. I decided to go back up to the porch outside my room for a while to look out over the ocean some more. As I sat there admiring the clear blue sky and the calm ocean waters, I found my thoughts drifting back to when I was at the bakery this morning. Sure, the donut was awesome, but that wasn't where my mind kept going. I kept thinking about the woman behind the counter, Kelly, who came out and waited on me. There was something about her that I couldn't get out of my head. Yes, she was certainly beautiful, with her light blonde hair and captivating eyes to the way she smiled and laughed, but there was more than that I found myself drawn to. The kindness she showed to me, a complete stranger to her, was not something you saw very often anymore.

I sat back in one of the reclining lounge chairs and slipped my sunglasses out of my shirt pocket and put them on. I looked up and could see a yellow kite flying off to just to the left. Someone was obviously having some fun down on the beach, a family perhaps, letting the kids laugh and control the kite, urging it on higher and higher. It brought me back to the times that my brothers and I would do the same thing while my mother sat under her big umbrella on the beach to keep the sun off her for the many hours we would spend running through the sand and water.

All this reflection made me realize just how lucky I have been since my childhood. I got to enjoy vacations with my family and probably had privileges that many other kids never got to experience because of the position my Dad held. I went to good private schools, got into Stanford and got my degrees in environmental sciences and then my MBA. I also got the opportunity to experiment, do intern work, and work on my invention ideas thanks to the opportunities I have had over the years. It was Dad's contacts that allowed me to get some of our first inventions introduced to big companies. I loved coming up with better ideas to clean up the ocean waters, get rid of oil and pollution, and even started work on the garbage islands and acres of trash out in the Pacific and in other locations.

Once those first inventions took off and did well with companies, it was making contacts with governments around the world that allowed us to really implement some change and give the oceans a chance. I was able to quickly build a staff of scientists, environmental specialists, business people and more, to the point where STW had over 5,000 employees around the world. I never thought that things would get so big, that I would oversee a huge corporation worth billions of dollars, but once it all started to happen, I found that I needed to make some changes in my life.

First, I needed to be careful about the people I had around me. Those closest to me have always said I was too trusting, too lenient, and too generous in my personal life. When it comes to business, I always felt cutthroat. It's almost like my business persona was a completely different person from who I was in my personal life. I had no problem giving speeches in front of hundreds of people, dealing toughly with heads of state or government offices, or even deciding to fire people if it calls for that. My personal life had always been much different. When I first started making good money, 'friends' were suddenly coming out of the woodwork, looking for help with this project or that, looking for investors, or offering help with managing things. I found myself doling out money in ways I probably shouldn't have. Finally, my father and brothers had a heart-to-heart conversation with me, telling me I needed to be more careful with what I was doing, looking out for people just hoping to take advantage of me. It was then that I realized they were right and had to take the rose-colored glasses off and be more observant and warier.

Even with all that, I still tried to be as helpful as I could. I worked with some charities, gave money while keeping it anonymous, and helped people where I could. For me, it has never about getting my name in the newspaper or good PR, though the public relations people I work with surely would wish I worked with them more. It was always more about helping people that needed it most, and giving people a chance that might otherwise not get the opportunity to get ahead or succeed.

I have had to sacrifice a great deal of my personal life to get ahead to where I am today, and I have had some regrets. I am sure there have been opportunities that have come along in my life, women that I have been with and had an interest in, that just didn't want to have to wait around all the time for me while I worked just to be with me. There were times when I was younger that I put work before my private life, and now that I was over thirty, I knew that it was more of a priority that I did not let life pass me by anymore. That was one of the reasons why I decided to buy the house when I did, and why I brought Shannon and James down here with me.

Both gave up a lot of their lives to work with me, and I began to feel guilty about how much they did for me. Yes, I paid them well and gave them bonuses and perks, but I wanted them to have time to enjoy life as well. I hoped a few weeks down here would help them to realize that and let them see that there should be more to life than just working with me.

After sitting and basking in the sunshine for a while, I decided to skip lunch and just go in and take a nap. I slid open the outside door to my room, shut it, and hopped onto the bed. I pressed the button on the side table that allowed me to control the blinds remotely so that I could darken the room easily. I then pressed another button to turn on the ceiling fan, so that it, combined with the air conditioning, would circulate some cool air through the room while I rested.

I couldn't even remember the last time I took a nap in the afternoon, but I have to say, it was wonderful. I just laid on the bed, pulling the cool down comforter up over me, and felt fantastic for the few hours that I managed to relax. When I awoke, it was hard to tell at first if it was still daylight or night out because the room was so dark. I forgot for a moment that I had control over the shades but then raised them so I could see that the sun was just starting to go down for the day.

Lazing around all day made me feel a bit restless, and I jumped up to put a pair of jeans on and a short sleeve, white button-down shirt. I walked out of my room and into the living room area, and all was quiet upstairs. I figured Shannon and James were probably downstairs hanging out, so I walked down the wood steps to the bottom floor. Sure enough, there they were, at the pool table, listening to some music and playing pool.

I walked over to the table just as James was sinking a bank shot. I could hear Shannon mumble a curse under her breath as she turned away from the table in disgust.

"Enjoying yourself, Shannon?" I asked her as I walked over to the bar where she was now sitting.

Shannon picked up the glass in front of her off the bar. I assumed it was her favorite gin and tonic with lime as she took a quick swig from the glass.

"I'd be having more fun if I could actually win a game from this guy," she said with a sneer.
James just looked up from the table and smiled as he sank another shot, gently tapping a colored ball into the far-right pocket.

"Shit!" Shannon yelled as she slammed her glass down.

James laughed as it was now an easy shot across the table to the eight-ball.

"Eight-ball, side pocket," he called, pointing to the side pocket with his cue.

James skittered the cue ball across towards the eight-ball, and the familiar clack knocked the ball right in.

"Well at least that's over with," Shannon said as she hung her cue back up on the rack with the others.

"Can we go get something to eat now that I have been embarrassed about losing three games in a row?" Shannon bemoaned. "We've been waiting for you to get up, Damian. I was ready to just leave you here, but James took pity on you and thought you might be hungry."

"Thanks, James," I said with a smile as I grabbed a beer from the fridge behind the bar. I popped the bottle open and tapped beer bottles with James.

James and I both sipped our beers while Shannon's eyes moved back and forth from one to the other.

"So?" she asked, showing her frustration at losing and her obvious hunger.

"Where do you want to go?" I asked her. "I don't really know of any of the places around here."
"I saw a place that looked good when we were driving in," James said as he finished his beer and tossed the bottle in the recycling bin. "It was right along the beach. It looked like a seafood, burger-type of place, maybe some good music playing. It was called The Dolphin's Cove."

"Sounds good to me," I told him. "Let's get going. I'm starved."

"Hold on, I just want to change quickly," Shannon said as she darted off into her room. James and I sat back down at the bar as I sipped some more of my beer.

"Had a good day?" I asked James as I took another sip.

"I think it was the first day I felt relaxed in a long time," he said to me with a smile. "After I washed the car, I wasn't quite sure what to do with myself. I worked out for a bit, which was great by the way, and just kicked back and watched the ocean for a while. It was awesome. Then Shannon got up and decided to challenge me to some pool. I had no idea she even played."

"Good," I replied. "I think we'll get to know a lot more about each other this vacation. The three of us spend a lot of time together, but it never seems relaxed or social. This will be fun."

Shannon came walking out of her room, wearing a short, light blue sleeveless dress with spaghetti straps. She slipped on her sandals and grabbed her purse and stood in the hallway, looking at the two of us staring at her.

"What?" she said, fixing her hair as if something was wrong.

"Nothing," I said to her as I got up from my seat. "I've just never seen you dressed this casually. You're always in a business suit. You look nice, right James?"
I gave James a nudge with my elbow to break him out of staring at Shannon.

"Yeah, nice," he said, coming back to reality.

"Well, thanks," Shannon said, feeling good about herself. "Now let's go; I need some food in me."

We walked out the front door and headed over to the garage. James pressed the remote for the garage, and the door slowly rose open. Inside were the cars I had sent down here. I'm not much of a car guy, but there were a few cars that I liked to own and wanted here. Besides the limo we had taken down here, I had a 1968 Ford Mustang convertible, 2018 Lexus LS, a Ford F-150, and a 1969 Mercedes-Benz 600 Pullman Limo.

"Holy shit," James said, looking at the cars. "When did you get these, and why haven't I been driving them?"

"The Mustang I've had for a while. The Lexus and the pickup truck I bought to have down here. The Mercedes is just something decadent that I wanted. I know it makes no sense to own something like that; I just thought it looked cool."

James ran his hand over the hood of the Lexus and looked back at me.

"Let's take this one tonight," he said to me, standing next to the driver's side door.

I went over and grabbed the key fob off a peg board in the garage and tossed it to him. I walked over and opened the front passenger side seat for Shannon, and she climbed in and sat next to James while I climbed in the back.

"Damian," James said after starting the car, "this car has no miles on it."

"I know," I told him. "I had the dealership truck it over yesterday, and they placed it in the garage."

James pulled the car out of the garage, and then I pressed a button on my phone using the app to close the garage door behind us. He slowly made his way up the street towards the gate, which slid open automatically as we approached it and then shut behind us.

James crept the car out onto the road and drove gingerly down the street, going the couple of miles it was to the restaurant while staying within the thirty miles-per-hour speed limit.

"Man, I wish we were someplace where I could open this thing up a bit," James lamented.

The restaurant came up on our right, all lit up and ready for us. The parking lot was crowded, but we were able to find a spot and then walked our way over to the restaurant across the gravel parking lot.

The restaurant jutted out a bit on a small pier so that it was over part of the ocean, and the bar had a mix of a classic beach place and tiki bar feel to it. I noticed as we were walking in that there was a sign for a band playing tonight – Captain Caraway and the Seeded Ryes. I chuckled when I saw the name and looked forward to seeing what they were like.

The place had a good crowd to it, with the restaurant area pretty full already. The hostess put us at a table in the bar area so we could listen to the band while we ate and drank, and we sat and ordered a round of drinks from our young waitress as she tried to speak loudly enough over the band doing their sound check.

Shannon had already picked up her menu and was going over it with precision, trying to find just what she wanted. James took a look and put his menu down right away, deciding quickly.

"You already know what you want?" Shannon asked him with shock.

"Shannon, look around at the place," he said, waving his hand. "It's a beach bar and restaurant. You come here and get seafood."

"I guess so," she said, still going over the menu to see if there was something better. James reached over and grabbed the menu from her and put it down.

"You know what you want, just go with what you thought of first. Otherwise, you'll be disappointed," James told her.

Our waitress came back over with our drinks, and we ordered, with James opting for a fish sandwich while I went with the crab cakes. Shannon, after much deliberation, finally decided on the shrimp scampi. I also ordered us some raw oysters to have before dinner.

"I've never had raw oysters," Shannon told us with a worried look on her face.

"Relax, they are tasty and easy to eat, " I told her as the band was getting started.

Captain Caraway was an older gentleman with gray hair tied back in a ponytail and a gray beard, but he also sported a hat much like what the Skipper wore on Gilligan's Island. The band jumped right into some cover tunes that everyone knew, and you could hear some people singing along.

The waitress came back with our tray of oysters served over ice. James went right for the hot sauce, dabbed some on one of the delicate oysters, and slid it right into his mouth, sucking it down. I took an oyster and did the same, and I could see that Shannon had a squeamish look on her face.

"Come on, Shannon," I said to her. "Just try one. You'll like it."

James picked up a shell with an oyster in it, spritzed it with some lemon juice and a bit of hot sauce, and handed it to Shannon.

"What do I do with it?" she said, looking at it confusingly.

"You slurp it down," James told her as he had another one.

"That's disgusting," she said, trying to hand it back to him.

"Give it a try," he said, pushing it back towards her.

Shannon took the shell in her hand and shakily held it up to her lips. She tilted her head back and let the oyster slide into her mouth and down. She then tossed the empty shell back on the plate and smiled.

"Okay, that was good," she admitted and grabbed another one.

It wasn't long before we had devoured all the oysters and ordered another round of them. After we polished off round two, our dinners arrived. The crab cakes were cooked to perfection and were delicate, with much more crab than filling, giving them the fresh, clean flavor that makes them spectacular. While I worked on the crab cakes, James chowed down his fish sandwich that was a golden brown from frying. Meanwhile, Shannon was enjoying her shrimp scampi, with the large, plump shrimp in the pungent garlic sauce over pasta. She alternated eating pieces of shrimp with sucking the pasta into her mouth like a little kid.

The three of us laughed and reveled in the music as the evening went on. It was the first time we had ever been out socially like that and we were having a great time. After our meal was done and cleared away, we ordered another round of drinks. James and Shannon decided to head over to the pool table and begin another round of their sports challenge for the night while I decided to sit and enjoy the band. I paid the check and kicked back, listening to the music.

As the band broke into "Under the Boardwalk," I looked up and over at the other side of the room where some of the small round tables were. Sitting there, gently swaying to the music, was Kelly from the bakery. She was dressed in just a white tank top and a pair of jeans, and I could see her hair down to her shoulders instead of the ponytail she had at the bakery.

She looked incredibly attractive, and I don't know what came over me, but there was a sudden thrust of boldness as I got up from the table and began to cross the room towards her table.

You better think of something to say before you get there, genius, my inner voice told me as I got closer and closer to her.

6

Kelly

Dinner at Mom's hadn't changed much at all since I was a kid living at home. Everything about the house pretty much looked the same to me. The ranch house was a great home to grow up in, and we always had lots of fun. Mom took dinner seriously, just like when we were kids, and made a special event out of it now when Jodie and I came over to eat. Why she thought we need a four-course meal all the time I'm not sure of, but I knew I appreciated that she went to the trouble to do it.

I arrived a few minutes before Jodie got there, and made sure to park my scooter in the driveway away from where she might knock it over when she came in. I walked in the front door and headed straight for the kitchen, where Mom already had steak and shrimp cooked and ready to put on the table. She was just finishing up getting green beans done when she spotted me.

"Kelly, grab the wooden salad bowl and throw together a salad for me, please," she asked as she strained the steamed green beans from the put and then tossed them with some butter and slivered almonds.

"You know Mom, we can come over for dinner one time and just have pizza, or burgers," I said as I reached up and grabbed the salad bowl from on top of the refrigerator.

"You worked hard all day, you deserve a good home cooked meal," Mom answered, ignoring what I said.

"You worked hard all day too. This is a lot of food for just the three of us."

"Why only three?" Mom asked as she finished with the green beans. "Is Jodie not coming?"

"No, she should be here in a minute," I told her as I stumbled for words. In my mind, I always assumed Alex was going to be late or skip dinner altogether to hang out at the beach with her friends.

Mom picked up her cell phone and sent a message to Alex. She put the phone down in a huff.

"Your sister better get here, or she's going to be grounded... again." Mom grabbed the bowl of green beans and placed them on the set table. Luckily, Jodie strode through the door a moment later, with Alex right behind her. I noticed Alex had made sure to put a t-shirt and shorts on to cover up her skimpy bikini.

"Look who I picked up before I left the beach," Jodie said with a smirk. Alex slinked over to the table and deposited herself in a chair.

Jodie came over to me as I put last touches on the salad.

"She was hanging out on the boardwalk with her girlfriends, flirting with some out-of-towners," she whispered to me. "I grabbed her and dragged her to the car."

"Smells great, Mom," Jodie said more loudly as she picked up the platter of steaks. I brought the salad over to the table and handed it to Alex before I sat down. Alex scooped some greens into her bowl and passed the salad right back to me, not even looking at me.

With everyone at the table, Mom made sure to say Grace before we started eating. She shot Alex a look to make sure she bowed her head in observance. Grace was one of the holdovers from when Dad was alive. It was something he always made us do before every dinner at the table as a way of showing respect and reverence.

We started off the meal quietly, eating our salads before passing around everything for the main course. It felt like it was five minutes before anyone broke the silence as we all ate quietly.

"How was the beach?" Mom said to Alex.

"Fine," she said with a huff, shooting an angry look to Jodie.

"I'll bet the water was warm this time of year," Mom answered, skewering a shrimp onto her fork.

"I never even got to the water," Alex pouted. "We hung out for a few minutes on the boardwalk and then Jodie manhandled me to get to her car."

Jodie laughed, nearly spitting green beans out of her mouth.

"I hardly manhandled you," she said in defense. "I just knew you would be screwed if you showed up late again."

"I would have made it here," Alex shot back.

"Not likely," Mom added, giving Alex a parental look. Alex put her head back down and went back to eating her meal.

"I thought maybe we could watch a movie after dinner," Mom said.

Jodie and I looked at each other because we knew where this was going. Mom always wanted to watch "Dirty Dancing," and we had probably seen the movie a hundred times by this time in our lives.

"Sorry, Mom," Jodie added. "Kelly and I are going out tonight."

"You are?" she said as she sat back in her chair.

"Yes," I said as I laid down my fork, trying to go along with Jodie. "We talked about it this afternoon, about how we never go out and do anything, blow off some steam."

"But you have to get up so early in the morning," Mom added.

"We won't stay out too late," Jodie remarked. "We'll probably still be in bed by eleven."

"Alone more than likely," Alex mumbled under her breath.

"Alexandra Rose!" Mom yelled. "We don't talk like that at the dinner table, or anywhere else in this house for that matter! Apologize to your sister."

"Sorry, Jodie," she said as she rolled her eyes when my Mom turned away. Jodie stuck her tongue out at her in response.

God, I love my sisters, I thought to myself, smiling proudly.

"You two are going out dressed like that?" Mom asked as she stood up, starting to clear the table.

"What's wrong with what I'm wearing?" I asked her.

"Well it's just a t-shirt and jeans," Mom said. "It's not very pretty."

"Thanks for the compliment, Mom," I told her as I grabbed the empty plates.

"I'm sure Alex has something we can borrow, she's not going anywhere anyway," Jodie said snidely.

"You're out of luck, Jodie," Alex answered. "Nothing I have will fit you. My boobs are way bigger than yours, and your ass is too big for my dresses."

Jodie squinted her eyes at Alex and walked over to her while Mom loaded the dishwasher.

"Would you like me to tell Mom how big your boobs look in your new bikini?" she whispered.

Alex' eyes widened. "I'm sure I can find something for the two of you. Come on in my room," Alex said as we left the kitchen and went down the hall to her room, formerly the room Jodie and I shared when we were growing up.

We walked into the room, and Alex shut the door behind us. Clothing was strewn all over the floor, the bed was unmade, and there was stuff everywhere you looked.

"How do you get away with your room looking like this?" I said to Alex as I picked up some clothes off the floor and tossed them into the empty hamper in her corner. "Mom would have killed us if we did this."

"I get away with it because Mom never comes in here," Alex said proudly. She walked over to her closet to see what she had that might fit Jodie. She grabbed a red dress off one of the hangers and handed it to Jodie.

"Try that one," Alex said. Alex went over to her dresser and opened the second drawer. She tossed out a couple of t-shirts onto the floor before finding what she was looking for.

"Here," she said to me, handing me a white tank top.

I pulled my t-shirt over my head and slipped the tank top on. It was a little roomy up top - *Alex really does have the bigger boobs,* I thought - but it was comfortable. It would go nicely with the jeans I had on.

Alex and I both looked over at Jodie, who was pulling the waist of the red dress down further, so it sat properly. The thin straps of the dress did nothing to hide the bra she was wearing, but the dress did look good on her, even if it was a little short.

"I can't wear this," Jodie answered, hooking her thumbs into the straps of her bra that were visible.

"Sure you can," Alex said, walking up behind her. Alex plunged her hands into the dress and unhooked Jodie's bra and then pulled it over her shoulders. Jodie reached in and pulled her bra out, and then adjusted the dress again.

"I never wear a bra with that dress," Alex said with a smile.

"I don't know how Mom ever lets you leave the house," I said to her.

"I have to admit, it looks pretty good," Jodie said as she gave a little twirl and looked at herself in the mirror. She adjusted the top portion again, making sure it was good enough, so one of her breasts didn't pop out every time she moved.

"Where are you two going?" Alex asked as she plopped down on her bed.
I looked over at Jodie, unsure just where we were going to go.

"Let's head over to Dolphin Cove. We haven't been there for a long time," Jodie said.

"Dolphin Cove?" I said to her. "That place will be crawling with vacationers. Can't we go someplace quieter?"

"You mean boring," Alex said to me.

"No, that's not what I meant, I just didn't want to come home with a headache is all."

"Kelly, the whole point of us going out tonight is to meet some new people. Going somewhere quieter means we won't meet anyone," Jodie said to me. "Now let's get going."

"Please take me with you guys," Alex pleaded.

"No way," I said. "You can't get in there unless you're twenty-one tonight anyway."

"I can pass for twenty-one," Alex said. "Please, I can't watch Dirty Dancing again tonight."

"Sorry kiddo," Jodie said, putting her arm around Alex. "It's a rite of passage for all of us. I used to beg Kelly to take me out with her to avoid it. Now it's your turn. Have the time of your life."

"You guys suck," Alex said to us as we walked out of the room.

"We're heading out, Mom," I yelled as we walked towards the front door.

Mom came out of the kitchen with a cup of tea in her hand. We could see the menu screen for the Dirty Dancing DVD she had frozen on the screen already.

"Okay, you girls have a nice time," she said to us. "Stay out of trouble. I'll see you in the morning."

Jodie and I walked out and over to her midnight blue Subaru and got in. It was a short drive over to the Dolphin Cove, and the Cove was probably one of the most popular bars in town. There were plenty of locations in and around the town, but since they were right on the water, a lot of the vacationers in the area flocked here for lunch, dinner, happy hour or entertainment.

We pulled in and parked and made our way up to the front door. I saw the sign that said Captian Caraway and the Seeded Ryes were performing tonight and rolled my eyes. Captain Caraway, also known as Nick Fisher, a local mechanic, had been performing in the area for many years. Nick loved the attention he got from being in the band, and even at fifty he still had his share of groupies.

Jodie and I nodded at the hostess as we walked in and pointed to a table over by the bar. We sat down at the raised round table, and a waitress came over to us, dressed in a tight t-shirt and shorts, to take our drink order. Jodie recognized her as someone she went to school with. They had a brief conversation about life in the area before she took our drink order. Jodie got a pina colada while I ordered a white Russian.

"Do you remember her?" Jodie said to me, trying not to be too loud but talking loud enough so I could hear her over the band playing "Margaritaville."

"No, I don't," I yelled back, "but I'm a few years older than you Jodie. You were a freshman when I was a senior."

"She was a great student, had a scholarship to college, then had to come home because her Mom got sick. She lost her scholarship, her Mom passed a couple of years ago, and now she's stuck here. Sometimes I worry that I'll end up that way too," Jodie said with a fretful look on her face.

"Jodie you never wanted to go to college. You always said you hated school," I said, surprised she felt this way.

"I know," she said. The waitress gave us our drinks, and we stopped talking until she left us alone again. Jodie took a sip of her drink. "Now though, as I get older, I think I should have gone. Part of me feels like I need to know more, that I could do better."

"You don't like working with me?" I asked her.

"Of course I like it, you doofus," she said to me. "But, and don't take this the wrong way Kel… I don't really work with you. I work for you. It's your business, not mine. If you decided to close up shop, move somewhere else, or something else happened, where would that leave me? I think I just need to have a better plan for my future."

"I never knew you felt this way," I said to her. "You know I don't look at it that way, right? I don't think of it as you working for me. We're a team, all four of us."

"Yes, but at some point, Mom is going to want to retire, Alex may go to college, or want to do something else, and then it's just you and me. I don't want you to keep the business going just because you worry about me, Kelly."

"I love the bakery, Jodie, and I want you to be part of it for as long as you want to be. Now let's stop talking about this depressing stuff. I thought we were coming out here to have fun and meet people," I told her. I held up my frosty glass, and she clinked hers against it as we both took long sips.

A moment later, there was a young, college-aged guy standing in front of our table. He was wearing a t-shirt and board shorts, had some wispy scruff of a beard, and spiky brown hair. He looked at me and smiled, and then turned his attention to Jodie.

"Hey there," he said to her, with a slightly Southern accent.

"Hi," she said to him, looking him over.

"Do you want to dance?" he asked her, bending over to speak into her ear.

The band was playing their cover of "Walking on Sunshine," an odd choice for a burly Captain Caraway, but they sounded pretty good. Jodie looked over at me and shrugged her shoulders.

"Go on," I said to her loudly.

She smiled and hopped off her stool, going out to the crowded dance floor with her hipster young man.

I sat on the stool, watching the dance floor, gently stirring the froth in my drink with my straw. The band finished up their song and started in with "Under the Boardwalk." I took a small sip just as someone walked up to our table and stood in front of me.

"Hi there," he said to me.

I didn't recognize the face and wondered if he was going to ask me to dance. He was a tall man with just a hint of stubble on his face, and he showed the faint beginnings of a tan as if he just arrived in town. I could see that he had strong arms showing beneath the short sleeve shirt that he wore.

"Hello," I said casually, turning my attention back to the band and spying Jodie dancing it up.

"You don't recognize me, do you?" he said to me with a smile.

"I'm sorry, no I don't. Do I know you?"

"Well, not really, I guess," he said as he sipped his beer.

I wondered where this guy was going with all of this and what his pickup line was going to be. I looked over at him, and he seemed like he was getting ready to say something or walk away, and he couldn't decide.

"I came into the bakery today," he said to me. "You gave me a donut because I didn't have my wallet on me to pay for it."

It dawned on me then who he was. He seemed flustered when I saw him this morning as well. I had thought he was cute at the time. Looking at him again in the dimmer lighting of the bar, he was more chiseled and manly than cute.

"Oh right, the jelly donut guy; I remember," I said to him, pointing at him. "I'm sorry, we get a lot of people coming through the shop this time of year."

"It's no problem," he said to me. "I just thought, since you were here that maybe I could buy you a drink as a way to say thank you for the donut."

"You don't have to do that," I said to him.

"Please, it's the least I can do," he said to me.

"Okay," I relented. "I would love another drink," I said as I slurped the last of my white Russian foam through my straw.

"May I sit?" he asked me.

I pointed to the empty stool to my right and nodded. The waitress came back over and asked if I wanted another, and I said yes. My guest also asked if he could get another beer.

As we sat and waited for the waitress to return, neither one of us had much of anything to say. It was funny that I never had a problem striking up a conversation with the people that came into the bakery each day, but when I was taken out of that setting, I never seemed to have much to talk about.

"The band's pretty good," he noted as they started the second verse of "Under the Boardwalk."

"Yeah, they've been playing around here for a long time. There something of legends in the area," I told him. I went back to fiddling with the paper umbrella I had taken out of my first drink. Thankfully the waitress arrived with our next round to break the awkwardness.

"Thank you for the drink," I said to him, raising my glass.

"Thank you for the donut," he said, lifting his beer bottle to touch my glass. We both took draws on our beverages.

"I'm Damian, by the way," he said to me. "I guess I probably should have introduced myself already," he said and followed it up with an uncomfortable laugh.
"I'm Kelly," I told him. "What brings you out to our town's hot spot tonight?" I was wondering if he was just a vacationer out trolling to see who he could reel in for the night.

"Just looking for a place to get something to eat, have a drink, and relax. My friends are over playing pool, and I saw you sitting here by yourself… I hope I'm not interrupting you."

I suddenly felt a warmth towards him and smiled at him.

"Don't worry about it, you're doing fine," I answered. "I don't often talk to guys outside of the bakery."

Damian seemed to relax a little bit after I said that and he laughed again.

Jodie came walking back over to the table, alone, and picked up her drink and finished it.
"That was fun," she said to me, not taking notice of Damian just yet. "That guy was just twenty-one and still in college. He's just a baby. I'm sure I could teach him a thing or two…"

I interrupted Jodie, tapping her on the arm.

"Jodie, this is Damian," I said to her pointing to Damian as he sipped his beer. "Damian, this is my sister, Jodie. She works with me at the bakery."

"Nice to meet you, Jodie," Damian said, extending his hand to her.

Jodie smiled at him and then looked at me and smiled.

"Well hello, Damian."

"Can I get you a drink, Jodie?" Damian asked her.
"That would be wonderful," she said to him, handing him her empty glass. "A pina colada, please."

"Be right back," he said as he walked up to the bar. Leaving us at the table.

"Where did he come from?" Jodie said as she looked at me.

"He came over to the table after you got up to dance," I said to her. "He had come into the bakery earlier today. I gave him a donut for free because he forgot his wallet."

"He's pretty handsome, Kelly. Good idea to give him a free donut."

"Stop it, Jodie. He's just being nice," I said to her, sipping my drink again.

"If he just wanted to be nice he would bring you a dollar tomorrow for the donut," Jodie remarked. "He wouldn't be buying us drinks unless he wanted to make an impression on you. You've been out of the dating pool too long."

Damian came back to the table with the drink for Jodie and handed it to her.

"Thanks," she said with a smile. "So Damian, are you here on vacation?" Jodie asked.

"Sort of," he said cryptically. "I'll be around for a few weeks. I came down here to relax with some friends. Actually, they are probably looking for me now since I wandered away from the table. I should probably get back to them."

I was feeling a little disappointed that he wouldn't be staying around longer.
"Thanks again for the drink," I said to Damian.

"It was my pleasure," he said, smiling at me. "I'm sure I'll be seeing you again. Your bakery was wonderful. I'll definitely be back in there, with money next time, I promise. It was nice to meet you, Jodie. Good night Kelly."

Damian gave a casual wave as we watched him walk away from the table. His jeans hugged his body perfectly, and I found myself staring like I hadn't stared at a man in a long while.

"Oh, you'll be seeing him again, Kelly," Jodie said with a laugh. "He's completely into you."

"I think you're reading way too much into this," I said to her.

Our waitress came back over to the table, and I asked her for the check so we could settle up.

"That guy who was with you paid your tab," she said to us. "Good guy. He paid for your drinks then gave me a fifty dollar tip. You can bring him around every weekend, Jodie."

Jodie turned back to me and grinned.

I looked over to where Damian had walked to, but there was no sign of him anywhere in the crowd.

Captain Caraway kicked in with "Caught Up in You" as Jodie and I grabbed our purses to head back out.

I hope I do see him again, I said to myself.

7

Damian

I wandered back over towards where our table was, glad I had got and gone over to Kelly, even if it was just to spend a few minutes talking with her. It gave me the start I needed, and I was sure I was going to make time to go and see her again tomorrow at the bakery.

James and Shannon still weren't back to our table, so I went over towards the back of the place to where the pool tables were to see if I could find them. Sure enough, there they were, laughing it up as James was getting ready to put the finishing touches on winning another game. James had just expertly knocked in the eight-ball with a series of tricky banks to win when I arrived at the table.

"Won again, I see," I said to James as I finished off my bottle of beer.

"He's like a Jedi master of pool," Shannon said, clearly miffed that she lost again. One thing about Shannon is she hates to lose, whether it is pool, the lottery, or anything to do with business.

"You ready to go, boss?" James asked as he hung up the pool cues and someone else moved towards the table.

"Whenever you guys are." I watched Shannon down the rest of her drink. She wobbled a little as she moved away from the pool table, and James quickly grabbed her arm to hold her up.

"Hold on there," James said, wrapping his arm around her waist to guide her. Shannon looked over at James and gave him a smile.

"I'm fine," she said to James but didn't push herself away from him either.

"I think now is a good time for us to go," I said to both of them. I saw the back door of the restaurant, and we decided to head out that way instead of working our way through the front. I had hoped to go out the front to see Kelly one more time, but it would have to wait until tomorrow.

James guided Shannon back over to our car in the lot, and she rested up against the side of the car while we got the passenger side open. James helped get her in her seat while I got in the back. As he leaned over her body to help her get her seat belt on, I saw Shannon lean into James' neck as if to give him a kiss.

"Hmmm, you smell nice," Shannon said to him as James pulled away and closed the door.

James got in behind the wheel and started the car to get us back home.

"How much did she have to drink?" I asked.

"Apparently more than she should have," James replied. "I thought she could handle her booze better than she can I guess."

"You know," Shannon said loudly, turning to face James, "I'm sitting right here. You could just ask me how much I had to drink."

"How much did you have to drink, Shannon?" I said to her.
"A lot, I guess," she said with a giggle.

Luckily it was just a short ride back to the house because no sooner had we gotten inside the gate and were headed towards the garage when Shannon yelled at us.

"Stop the car, I have to puke," she said as she opened the passenger door just short of the garage. James slammed on the brakes and seconds after the door opened I could hear Shannon spewing vomit onto the driveway.

"Well, that will be fun to clean up in the morning," James said with a sigh.

Shannon and I got out of the car as James finished pulling the Lexus into the garage. I kept a close eye on her to make sure she was okay, and she did drift a few steps as she threw up one more time in one of the bushes outside the front steps.

"You okay?" I asked her, putting my hand on her back.

Shannon looked up at me, her eyes barely open, with a small trail of saliva running down her chin.

"Peachy," she said to me as she turned and threw up again.

James came out of the garage to meet us and helped Shannon up the front steps as I opened the door and shut off the alarm.

"I'm going to get her into her room," James said to me as I followed them down the hall.

"Good idea."

I watched James open her door and take her inside. I walked down the hall and into the game room, going to the bar to make myself a vodka martini. By the time I had shaken the martini and poured into my glass, James was walking over towards the bar to sit with me.

"All taken care of?" I asked him.

James laughed a little.

"Yeah, she's in bed," he said to me. "I've never seen Shannon like that before. It was kind of fun to see her loosen up a bit, but she'll be feeling it in the morning."

"No doubt." I took a sip of my martini, feeling the cool, crisp vodka on my lips.

"Oh, I almost forgot. "James got up from the bar and went back down the hall. Moments later, he appeared with a basket in his hands. He placed the wicker basket down on the bar. I could see it was filled with various pastries and treats.

"What's this?" I said to him, looking at the basket.

"A couple of ladies dropped it off this afternoon while you were sleeping," James said to me. "They said they were from the local bakery on the boardwalk and wanted to welcome you to the neighborhood. It's pretty good stuff; I had a muffin from there this afternoon. Shannon had it put in her room. I think she was hoping to snitch what she wanted before you got it."

"Were the ladies a couple of blondes, about the same height, one with big brown eyes?" I asked him.

"Well, they were blondes, but I didn't notice anything about their eyes. One of them kept staring at me the whole time."

"I was at the bakery this morning," I said to James as I reached into the fridge and grabbed a beer for him. "And I saw them at the restaurant tonight. In fact, I went over and talked to the one with the big brown eyes when I saw her."

"Really?" James said as he took a draw of his beer. "They both were pretty cute, but it sounds like you are more interested in Brown Eyes."

"Her name is Kelly," I said to James. "And yes, I am interested. There was something about her when I first saw her at the bakery. I wish I had gotten to talk to her longer tonight, but her sister was there with her, and it seemed like she was looking for a way out of there."

James almost spit out some of his beer from laughing.

"What's so funny?" I asked indignantly.

"I'm sorry, boss," James said as he wiped his chin. "It's just hard for me to imagine that you get flustered about talking to anyone. You talk to CEOs, presidents, heads of state, and thousands of people all the time without any trouble. You're telling me a petite blonde throws you off?"

I picked up a chocolate chip cookie from the basket and bit into it. It was just the right texture, the right amount of softness with the perfect number of chips in the bite.

"We're not all as tough as you are, James," I said to him, taking another bite of the cookie.

James reached into the basket and grabbed one for himself, taking a big bite out of it.

"Wow, these are good," he said to me. "So, are you going to go see her again? It would probably be gentlemanly of you to go and say thanks for the basket."

"It does give me the perfect excuse to stop by there again in the morning," I told James. "The only problem is that they are so busy in there that I am sure I won't get time to talk to her. She's the owner, and I think she works in the kitchen mostly. I could go there, and she might not even be able to speak to me."

James took a long sip of his beer and placed the bottle down on the bar.

"Do you want me to walk you through this?" James asked me.

"What are you talking about? I don't need you to hold my hand and take me there, James, if that's what you mean."

"That's not what I meant," he said. "I can give you some pointers though about how to approach everything. It sounds like you might need some help."

"I don't need to get tips about talking to women."

"You're right, you shouldn't," James replied. "But it looks like you do. Look, you want to make a good impression on this woman, right? Then you want to make sure you seem confident when you go to talk to her. Just be yourself and relax about it. You don't have to get yourself all worked up. Go in, thank her for the basket, and ask her if you can take her out somewhere for dinner, or drinks, or something else."

"I realize this shouldn't be a big deal for me," I said to James. "So why do I have a knot in my stomach just thinking about it?"

James smiled at me again after he finished his beer.

"I know you just met her, but she obviously has struck a nerve with you. Sometimes it happens that way when you are attracted to someone."

I glanced over at James with a serious look on my face.

"It's been a long time for me since I have found anyone I was attracted to right away like this, maybe since I was in college. I don't want to seem like a bumbling idiot and blow it right off the bat."

"You'll do fine," James said as he stood up and yawned. "I think I am going to head off to bed. I'll check in on Shannon to make sure she is okay. Hopefully, she's just sound asleep already."

"Goodnight, James, and thanks," I said to him, raising my glass.

"No problem, boss," he said to me, giving a wave before heading down the hall.

I polished off the rest of my drink, rinsed the glass in the bar sink and left it to dry. I walked back down the hall and could hear loud snoring coming from Shannon's room. I laughed to myself as I went by and headed up the stairs, trying to do so quietly so I wouldn't wake her. I was pretty sure Shannon was going to be miserable in the morning.

I got to the top floor, and instead of going into the bedroom I went outside onto the patio to sit for a bit. The wind had picked up a little bit, and I could see some lightning in the clouds off in the distance out over the ocean. A storm was moving in that hopefully would cool off some of the humidity that was around right now. I could hear the waves picking up and hitting the beach more strongly than they had earlier in the day. I walked over to the railing and looked down and could see the outside portion of the pool with its solar lighting around it dimly lighting the area. The lights gave off enough that I could just see out onto the beach a few yards. I could hear the echoes of some kids running along the beach further down, and there was a hint of flashlights moving off in the distance.

My thoughts turned back to my brief interactions with Kelly today and how much I enjoyed seeing her and speaking with her. I knew I wanted to see more of her and hoped she felt the same way about me. Now it was going to be a matter of making it happen.

8

Kelly

I'm not sure how long my alarm was going off for, but Alice had stopped waiting patiently for me to get out of bed and was now licking my face and breathing heavily on me, making sure I would pry my eyes open and notice her. When I looked at my clock and saw it as 4:15; I jumped up out of bed, let Alice out the back door, and then took the fastest shower I had taken in a long time to get myself ready for the day. By the time I was dressed and had let Alice back into the house, it was creeping closer to 5 AM, and I knew I had to get going.

Sundays were often the busiest days at the bakery as people were coming and going from the rental homes for the week and looking for an easy place to grab some breakfast. The locals knew they could get their Sunday treats as well for their after-church meals. We usually had a steady stream of customers from 7 AM right through to closing, so getting everything prepared early was key to helping the day go well. Me showing up late was not part of the plan.

I sped over to the bakery on my scooter, getting it moving as fast as I could. That included making a few nifty maneuvers along the way to avoid a turtle I saw at the last minute working its way across the road. I got to my usual parking spot, locked up, and quickly climbed the steps to the back entrance. I pulled the door and it sprang open, letting me know Mom had arrived before me and unlocked the place to let everyone in.

"Sorry I'm late," I shouted out as I pulled my apron on to get things started. Jodie, Alex, and Mom were all involved in their tasks for the morning, but they looked over at me as I washed up and pulled some gloves on to start working.

"What's wrong?" I asked as I saw them all staring at me.

"Nothing," Alex noted as she got ready to put some cookies in the oven. "Jodie was just telling us about your night last night."

"What about it? We had fun, and it was a good night out to decompress a bit."

"She was talking more about Damian, " Alex shot me a grin as she bumped one of the oven doors closed with her hip.

"Who?" I responded, trying to concentrate more on getting the pastries ready to start baking. It was then it dawned on me just who they were talking about.

"You remember," Jodie added. "The handsome guy who bought our drinks last night. The one who was chatting you up and flirting with you."

"I would hardly call it flirting, Jodie." I kept working at some of the dough, probably more vigorously than I needed to, while trying to concentrate on work.

"He said he was going to stop back in," Jodie said as she came over and stood next to me. " If he shows up this morning, then you'll know for sure if he just likes donuts or if he has something else in mind."

"Can we get to work please and stop worrying about who will or won't come in this morning? We have to open in ninety minutes and have a lot of work to do," I said curtly, hoping to get everyone focusing on something other than my social life.

"Yes, Ma'am," Jodie said, snapping to attention.

Mom and Alex started loading up the display cases and got everything ready for the coffee service while Jodie and I kept working on baking. I was sure Jodie could see I was a little put off by all the ribbing this morning.

"Hey, Kelly, relax. I was just teasing you," Jodie said to me. "You're taking this way too seriously."

"Me? You're the one who felt the need to talk about it to everyone. So some guy bought me a drink and talked to me. You were out there dancing and flirting, and no one was talking about that."

"Because that's what I do all the time," Jodie told me. "You rarely go out and when you do you don't talk to anyone but me. You talking to a guy is news in this family. Stop getting all bent out of shape about it. I'm your sister; I'm allowed to give you a hard time. It's my job."

I exhaled deeply and looked at Jodie.

"Okay, I'm sorry. Now can we get back to baking please?"

"You're going to be a joy to work with today. That's the last time I take you out on a work night," Jodie mumbled under her breath.

I pushed my way through the prep work, focusing on the tasks we had before the doors open so we were ready for the crowds. Everyone just let me be in the kitchen, and when the shop got busy, Jodie even volunteered to go out and help instead of me going, which let me press on so we could turn out more goodies. I could hear how busy it was out in the shop and peeked out once to see what was going on and there was a line that stretched nearly out the door.

The mob scene went on for a few hours after we opened, depleting our supplies in the shop quickly. We had enough to replenish the things like donuts and pastries to keep up with demand for a Sunday, but it meant staying on top of things in the kitchen to keep turning out what people were looking for.

By about 10:30, things had slowed down enough where there were just a few people coming in and out. Most visitors had left town by then, and the new batch that was coming in for the week were staking their claims to their rental homes or condos, doing their food shopping, and then hitting the beach to make the most of the warm day. The occasional person would stroll in now looking for an iced tea or iced coffee, or a quick snack for the kids they had in tow.

I did some straightening up in the back and looked at what ingredients I would need to order for the coming week before placing orders using my tablet as I moved along. Mom came into the kitchen, carrying an iced coffee for me.

"Thanks," I told her as I grabbed the cup and took a long sip.

"It was pretty crazy out there this morning," Mom commented as she straightened up. She could never stand still for a second.

"That's a good thing." I sipped more of the coffee, draining half of it.

"Jodie's taking a look to see what has sold well and what hasn't. Maybe we should add some blueberry turnovers next week to go with the apple," Mom said as she grabbed the broom from the corner and started sweeping up some of the flour.

"Mom, that can wait until later," I said, walking over and grabbing the broom from her hand. "Why don't you give yourself a break and go sit at one of the tables?"
I started walking her out of the kitchen and led her to one of the empty tables. I sat down with her, with my back to the door. Just as I sat for a second, I heard the bells on the door jingle as someone came in. I looked up and saw Damian standing there.

He was dressed in a pair of board shorts and a Hawaiian shirt. He pulled off his sunglasses and folded them, stuffing them in his shirt pocket so that I could see his deep blue eyes.

"Good morning," he said with a smile.

"Hi there," I replied, picking up my iced coffee and slurping it loudly now that it was nearly empty.

Not only was Mom looking over at Damian, but I noticed Jodie and Alex both stopped what they were doing to watch our interaction. I suddenly felt like I was on stage with everyone watching what I would do.

"Come in for another donut?" I asked him as I stood up, brushing some of the flour off myself.

"I would love one if you have any left," he said as he walked towards the display case.

All eyes followed us as we moved, and I got behind the counter and reached over and grabbed the last jelly donut from the display case.

"You're in luck, the last one." I placed the donut in a white paper bag. "Anything else?"

"Actually, yes." Damian reached into his wallet and pulled out a dollar bill. "This is for the donut yesterday."

"Damian, you don't have to," I said, holding my hand up. "You bought our drinks last night, which was more than generous of you."

"I was happy to do it, but that was before I knew about the basket."

"What basket?" I said with some confusion.

"The basket you and your sister delivered to my house yesterday," he said to me. "It was filled with all kinds of treats. James told me you two dropped it off. It was very nice of you. We have been snacking on it."

I wasn't sure how to respond. Jodie was now standing next to me to get closer to the conversation.

"You're Mr. Woods?" Jodie asked since I hadn't said anything.

"I am," Damian answered. "I guess I didn't mention it last night."

"The guy with the giant house at the end of the boardwalk?" Alex added as she walked over. "Man, you must be loaded."

I shot Alex a look and Mom came over right away.

"Alex, come and help me in the kitchen," she said, whisking her quickly away through the kitchen door.

"Is everything okay?" Damian asked me. I was still in kind of a shock. Damian looked nothing like the Mr. Woods I had envisioned and certainly didn't act like I thought he would.

"It's fine," I finally blurted out. "You're just not... not what I expected I guess."
"Oh?" he questioned. "What were you expecting?" I could see he was more than a little curious as to how I would answer that.

"I don't know... I mean we get lots of people buying big houses around here, and they're... "

Damian interrupted me.

"Fat, old guys with lots of money that are demanding and rude?"

I could feel myself starting to blush.

"It's okay," he said with a laugh. "I know plenty of people that are just like you were thinking. I don't like dealing with them either."

Damian placed two dollars on the counter to pay for his donut yesterday and for the one today. I mindlessly picked them up and rang them into the register and then handed him the bag. Damian held the bag in his hand for a second, not pulling it away from me.

"I know you're probably pretty busy here most of the time, but I saw on the door it says you close at three. If you would like to come to the house today when you're finished here, I would love to have you over for dinner."

I couldn't believe he was asking me out on a date, and inviting me to his house no less. I stood there with my mouth open a little, not knowing what to say. I felt Jodie's foot slide over and step on mine to break my trance.

"I... I don't know, we have cleaning and prep work..." I said trying to come up with excuses.
"Alex, Mom and I can handle the cleaning tonight, Kelly," Jodie said to me. "And besides, we're closed tomorrow, so you don't have to get up early."

I shot Jodie a look as she backed me into a corner.

"Great," Damian said to me. "So you can come?"

"I guess I can," I said through my teeth, still looking at Jodie. I turned back to Damian and saw him smiling at me and could feel myself melt a bit.

"Perfect, come by any time you're ready." Damian took his donut from me. "It was nice to see you again, Jodie," Damian told her as he turned and walked out the door. My eyes followed him all the way out until he walked past the front window and on his way.

"Holy shit, Kel!" Jodie exclaimed, pushing me slightly.

I shook my head and walked back into the kitchen, where Mom and Alex were putting some cookies on trays to refill the cases.

"What happened?" Alex said as I walked over to the counter and went back to kneading some of the dough I had taken out to warm up to room temperature.

"Kelly is going on a date tonight," Jodie said with a smile.

"With the billionaire?" Alex yelled.

I just kept working the dough back and forth, tossing it over and folding it, trying to block the conversation out.

"Yep. She's going to his house for dinner tonight."

"Kelly, you are so lucky," Alex said to me, coming over to stand next to me. "Make sure you take pictures of the house."

"I am not going to do that, Alex. I don't know that I even want to go."

"Why wouldn't you want to go?" Jodie asked me. "You said yesterday you wanted to see inside the house and then let him have it about how over the top it is and how he's spoiling the beach for everyone. Now you have the opportunity to do it. You have dinner, see the house, and then say your piece. Unless you feel differently about him now that you have seen him and talked to him."

"There's lots of work to do around here," I said. "I have to get next week's orders in, plan what we are going to make, think about any cake orders we have coming up. I can't just leave all that stuff. I have a business to run."

"It's one night, Kelly," Jodie said to me. "Mom and I can plan next week and place the orders for you. Go have dinner with him. If you have a good time, then that's great. If you find out he's the self-centered dud you thought he would be, then let him have it and walk out. You have nothing to lose."

"I'll go, I'll go," I said, wanting to move on from all this.

"You're not going dressed like this are you?" Alex added.

"What's wrong with how I look?" I said defensively.

"Kelly, the guy's a billionaire. He probably dates actresses and fashion models all the time. You want to make sure you look amazing, so he takes notice of you, not go schlepping in there in your jeans and t-shirt with your hair a mess."

"Two of the three times he's seen me have been in here when I am schlepping around in jeans and an apron. If he can't handle that I look like this most of the time, that's his problem, not mine. See, that's just another reason for me not to do this," I said as I took off my gloves and tossed them in the garbage.

"Don't listen to either of them, Kelly," Mom said to me. "If he really likes you, he doesn't care what you wear or how you look right when you get there. He seemed like a nice gentleman that just wants to get to know you. If you're unsure about it, don't go. It's not the end of the world."

"It is the end of the world if you pass up the chance to date a billionaire!" Alex yelled. "You'll never get another chance like this. Go home and put something nice on, or better yet go to my closet and put something sexy on that will make his eyes pop out."

"Alexandra!" Mom scolded. "Kelly, don't get pressured into anything you aren't comfortable with."

I heard the front door open and close and went out into the store to wait on the customer. I needed to get away from all three of them so I could decide for myself what to do. After giving the customer the last of the peanut butter cookies, I sat down on the stool behind the register.

Jodie came out shortly after to stand next to me.

"Look, Kelly, Mom's right," she said. "If you don't want to go, forget about it. But I can tell part of you is at least curious to see what he's all about. There's no denying there was some attraction between the two of you. I saw it last night."

I got up from the stool and walked back toward's the kitchen door.
"Where are you going?" Jodie asked with exasperation.

"I'm making another batch of peanut butter cookies," I told her. "And then I am going to Damian Woods' house to see what he's all about."

I pushed open the door, confident I was making the right decision for me.

9

Damian

I strolled back towards the house, happy with the notion that Kelly was willing to come over after work and have some dinner. As I walked along, I came to the realization that I didn't know if I had anything to cook for dinner tonight. Sure, the fridge had some stuff in it, but I wanted to make sure I made a good impression on her. How could I make a good impression though if I didn't know what she liked? Should I make steak? Chicken? Pasta? What if she was vegetarian or had a gluten intolerance? I quickly found myself worrying about what to make the closer I got to the house.

I walked into the house and didn't hear Shannon or James down on the first floor. To be honest, I thought Shannon might just sleep all day after the night she had last night. When I got up to the second floor, I walked over towards the exercise room to see if James was in there. He was nowhere to be found, but I did hear someone in by the pool. When I opened the door, there he was, swimming some laps and, to my surprise, Shannon was there, curled up on a lounge chair, sunglasses firmly planted over her eyes. The sun was shining brightly over the indoor portion of the pool, so I didn't blame her for having them on.

"Good morning… actually good afternoon," I said to her after I glanced at my watch.

"If you say so," she muttered.

"How are you feeling?" I asked her as I sat in the chair next to her.

"Like I got hit by a bus, and then a squirrel came over and died in my mouth."

"Powerful image, Shannon," I said to her. I opened the paper bag I was carrying and took out the jelly donut.

"Want a bite?" I asked her, holding up the side of the donut with jelly gently oozing out.

"Ugh, no food," she said, holding up her hand and pushing the donut away.

"Your loss," I said as I took a big bite.

I polished off the donut in three quick bites, licking the sugar off my fingers while Shannon looked on in disgust.

"Why did you even get out of bed yet if you feel so crappy?"

"I would have stayed in bed if Michael Phelps here didn't make me get up to keep him company. He plied me with coffee, water, and aspirin if I sat here while he swam."

James had just finished up his last lap and made his way up the pool steps and over towards us. He grabbed a towel nearby and started to dry off before coming over and sitting down.

"Hey boss," he said to me. "The pool is great. The water feels perfect." James looked over and saw the empty bag on the table.

"So, you went to the bakery today, I see," James said to me, smiling. "How did it go?"

"It went well. In fact, I invited Kelly over for dinner tonight."

Shannon sat up in her chair and whipped off her sunglasses, revealing her dark, bloodshot eyes.

"Who's Kelly? What happened at the bakery? What am I missing?"

"The boss ran into one of the ladies who brought the basket over yesterday at the restaurant last night and hit it off with her. He went back this morning to say thanks, and I guess now they have a date," James told Shannon, bringing her up to speed.

"How did all this happen without me knowing about it?" Shannon said to me.

"Well, you were not really in the condition to talk about it last night when it happened," I told her. "Now that you two know about this, I need to ask you both for a favor."

James and Shannon both looked at me, wondering where this conversation was going.

"Actually," I continued, "I need two favors. I need to get something to make for dinner tonight. I don't think we have anything not frozen that I could make for tonight."

"That's easy enough," James said. "We can run out and get something or call the home care service and see if they can deliver something for you. What's the second favor?"

I looked at both of them seriously.

"I need you two to leave the house, just for a few hours. I hate to ask, but it might be weird if you guys were here, at least this first time."

"Oh come on, Damian," Shannon cried out. "You know I feel like crap today. Can't I just lock myself in my room and stay there if I promise to stay quiet? I really don't want to go out any place."

I turned my attention to James, hoping he would be on my side and give me some help.

"Come on Shannon," James said to her, "it's the least we can do for him. You said it yourself – the guy hasn't had a real date in months. Let's give him a chance to have some space. I'll take you anywhere you want to go. We can even take the limo if you want."

"Anywhere I want, huh?" Shannon said, a twinkle of interest in her eyes now. "Okay, I'll go, but you owe me big, Damian. And we're not taking the limo. You can't maneuver that thing on these little streets. Let's take the Mustang, and I want to drive."

James and I looked at each other, and both sighed.

"Fine, you can drive," James said with resignation.

"Great." Shannon bounced out of her lounge chair, seemingly filled with life again. "I'm going to get myself ready, and I'll call the service and see what I can arrange for them to bring over. James, go get yourself cleaned up and get ready to spoil me."

We both watched Shannon march off and out of the pool area.

"I have a feeling I am going to regret doing this," James said to me.

"Thanks, James. I owe you big time. I promise I'll make it up to you."
"Don't worry about it." James wrapped the towel around his waist and made for the door.

"I better go get myself ready since I have no idea what I am in store for now."

I followed James out the door and went upstairs to start getting myself ready for Kelly. I wasn't sure what time she might show up beyond knowing it would be after three. I went and jumped in the shower, making sure to shave off the stubble that had grown over the last two days. I decided I didn't want to get too dressed up and just put on a white linen shirt and some khaki shorts. By the time I had finished getting ready and made my way out to the kitchen, Shannon and James were both sitting out in the living room area waiting for me.

"You're all set," Shannon said to me. "They'll be a delivery here in about twenty minutes with the food. The rest is up to you."

"Thanks, Shannon," I said to her.

Shannon got up from the couch and turned to James.

"Okay, let's hit the road," she told him.

James got up from the couch and walked over toward me.

"So where are you going?" I asked him.

"I have no idea," he said to me as he shrugged his shoulders. "She hasn't said anything to me. It's all a surprise I guess."

"Well, just use the Amex card for anything, and I'll cover it. Do you need cash?" I asked him.

"I'm good, boss," he said, waving me off.
"Man, I can't wait to get behind the wheel of that Mustang," Shannon said with excitement.

"If I need you to bail us out, I'll give you a call," James said as Shannon tugged him towards the stairs.

"Enjoy your date, Damian!" Shannon yelled as I heard them go down the stairs and eventually heard the front door slam. A few moments later, I could hear the roar of the Mustang engine coming from below me and then heard the tires squeal, no doubt after the gate opened so Shannon could pull the car out.

The house was suddenly very quiet, and I put some background music on just to help break things up and help me relax a bit. It was just a few minutes later when I heard the buzzer, indicating someone was at the gate. I glanced over at the monitor to see if it was Kelly, but it was a white van from the delivery service. I buzzed them in so they could pull up to the house, and then used the remote to unlock the front door when they arrived, directing them to use the elevator to bring things up.

I heard the ding of the elevator as they reached the top floor, and out walked two men all dressed in white. One was carrying a large pot, and the other had a couple of bags that he placed on the kitchen counter. Shannon had ordered a clambake for two, and the one gentleman gave me some quick direction on how everything should be prepared. They had also brought along some wine, appetizers, and dessert in case I needed them. I made sure to tip them both well, thanking them profusely for the help, and then hustled them out the door so they would be gone before Kelly arrived.

I put the items in the refrigerator to keep them cold, and I could hear the lobsters scratching away at the cooler they were in as I stored them for the moment. I took some time to set up the small table that was positioned nearest to the windows that looked out over the ocean so that the setting was nice, putting some candles on the table that I could light later.

When everything was done, I took a quick look at my watch and saw it was after four. I began to wonder if Kelly had changed her mind and decided not to come after all. I tried not to get too tense about it and walked over to the bar and made myself a vodka martini. I had just finished pouring the drink into my glass when the sound of the buzzer cut through the silence in the room.

A glance at the monitor showed Kelly standing at the gate, waiting for a response.

10

Kelly

I thought about riding my scooter over to the Damian Woods "compound," but I figured I wasn't going to be there long enough for me to have to worry about walking back to get the scooter to go home. As I marched down the boardwalk, my hair still wrapped in my ponytail, I could feel my resolve building to go into the house, see what was there, and then let Damian know what I thought of him building his monstrosity on the beach and how selfish and pretentious he was. After I had my say, I could turn around and walk out, go get my scooter and go home and I have a nice glass of wine, reveling in the look that would be on his face when he got schooled by a local.

I got to the end of the boardwalk and went down the steps, taking me over to the road that led down to his front gate. Suddenly I had butterflies in my stomach. I was nervous, not so much about what I had wanted to say to Damian, but if things turned out differently, I didn't think I was sure how I would react. There was no denying he was nice and friendly from the interactions I had with him, and he certainly was someone I was physically attracted to.

I walked slowly towards the gate and could feel myself sweating more as I got closer with each step. Beads formed on my forehead as the sun beat down on me, and I felt like I was breathing a bit heavier than I should have been.

Maybe this is a bad idea, I said to myself as I got about twenty yards from the gate.

I stopped and looked at the giant house looming in front of me behind the iron fence. If I was going to do this, one way or the other, this might be the only opportunity I had. I shuffled along the sandy road until I stood in front of the entrance and reached over to press the buzzer. My hand shook slightly and hesitated.

I could hear myself say "to hell with this," and got ready to turn and go, but then my index finger seemed to jump on its own and hit the buzzer. I thought about turning and running, but my legs and my brain were not on the same page at this point either. I tried to remain calm and stand still, figuring there was a camera somewhere that was pointed at the entrance, watching me. My left foot started to tap as I waited for a response.

"Hold on one second," Damian's voice crackled over the intercom.

The gates slowly hummed and retracted, and I began my descent down the driveway. The black limo was still parked just where it was yesterday when we saw James out washing it, making me wonder if there was a houseful of servants inside to wait on Damian's every whim. I knew if I saw that it would give me one more reason not to stay very long.

By the time I reached the front steps, Damian had opened the front door and was standing there waiting for me.

"I'm glad you could make it," Damian said to me, holding the door open for me as I slid past him and went inside.

The cool blast of the air conditioning enveloped me as soon as he shut the front door, sending shivers up and down my body.

We stood in front of the staircase for a moment, neither one of us sure as to what to do next.

"I guess you didn't have any trouble finding the place," Damian said, a lame attempt at a joke.

"It's kind of a hard place to miss," I told him, only half-joking myself.

"I know, the place seems a little... ostentatious, I guess. When we were working out the plans for everything, and I saw the final blueprints, I was a little worried about how everyone would react to the house. Would you like the grand tour?"

"Do we have enough time to see it all before dinner?" I cracked.

"I think we can squeeze it all in," Damian told me as he started walking down the hall.

I followed along, looking at the artwork on the walls, typical beach stuff with shells and driftwood that tourists often go for when decorating rental homes. We walked past a few rooms with closed doors that I assumed were bedrooms either for guests, or staff, or both. We ended up in an immense room with a pool table, big screen TV, a large bar and a jukebox.

"Wow, quite a space," I said, knowing I sounded unimpressed. I moved towards the center of the room and saw another small hallway beyond where the TV was mounted.

"What's down there?" I asked.

"Oh," Damian answered. "There's a laundry room and a small movie theater in the other room."

"Fancy," I told him. "I see you have an elevator too."

"Just easier to bring bags up and down that way," Damian replied nonchalantly. "Come on," he told me, leading me back down the hall to the staircase so we could go up to the second floor.

I could see bedroom doors to my left and right, but down at the end of the hall were large clear windows. We walked towards the area, and before we got there, I could see rooms on either side.

"This room is the fitness room," Damian said pointing to the left.

I peeked in and saw the room filled with various workout equipment, all top-of-the-line stuff, and some TV screens so you could watch while you worked out.

"And this is another fitness room," he said, heading off to his right. This room was a little larger and was outfitted with a boxing ring, heavy bags, and other equipment.

"You have your own boxing ring?" I said to him.

"I like to box for my workout, so I thought it would be useful."

"Who do you box?" I asked, thinking he probably had designated people that come in for him to punch.

"Well, I hadn't really thought about it that much," Damian said, feeling sheepish. "James and I do spar sometimes."

We walked back out, and I was standing before the pool area. Damian opened the door for me, and I went in. The transition from the cool, air-conditioned house to the warm air around the pool hit me square in the face. I could hear my sneakers squeaking on the floor as we moved closer to the pool. I saw the area on the far wall where the pool had a small transition to the outdoor area.

"Nice," I said to him, trying to sound casual. "I have to tell you, Damian, having a pool at the beach seems a little… well strange to me."

Damian looked back at me as if he were expecting me to say something like this.

"I know," he told me. "I'm sure people around here just think I'm some eccentric rich guy that doesn't want to swim in the ocean. Truth is I love the ocean and love to swim in it. I just thought some of my friends and family would like the pool better, especially the kids."

"Did it have to be indoors and outdoors?" I asked him. I could tell my questions were starting to make him feel a little uncomfortable. Part of me felt victorious in my efforts, and another a little guilty for pressing him so much.

"No, it didn't have to be, but I thought it looked nice," he said honestly. "Besides, now I can swim even if the weather isn't so good in the summer or the winter."

"So, you plan to be down here often?"

"Yes," he said, standing in front of me now. "I plan on making this area my home, maybe even full-time if I can work it out."

"Hmmm," I said to him as I looked out on the vast pool area outside.

"You sound skeptical of my intent," he said to me as we started walking back to the entrance to the indoor pool area.

"Well, we have lots of rich folks come down here and build houses or buy houses with the same idea, but I think once they see what life is like living here, they get a little bored with it and change their minds. There's not much of a nightlife here, and even less so in the winter."

I walked back into the air conditioning, grateful to have the cool air on me again.

"I can see that," Damian said as we started to climb the steps to the next floor. "But I'm not much for going out on the town. I do a lot of that stuff because I must. I don't go in for art shows, restaurant openings, and red carpets. That stuff bores me. I'm more of a homebody."

We reached the top floor, which was perhaps the most expansive in the house. Each room was nicely decorated, and the kitchen Damian had seemed larger than the one I had in the bakery. It was an open floor plan, so all the rooms melded together nicely, and there was one room with a closed door that I assumed was his bedroom. I walked over to the glass doors that opened onto the patio outside and opened them to step out and have a look. It felt like I was far above the beach, and I could see the beach out to the right and where public access opened up again about fifty yards down. Just below us was the outdoor pool, with a waterfall and slide, a cabana outside, and what looked like a built-in stone grill and other outdoor accessories.

"Can I get you something to drink?" Damian called to me from inside.

I turned toward him and saw him standing behind the bar, ready to get me anything I could ask for.

"A glass of white wine would be nice, please," I said to him as I looked back out over the ocean.

I had grown up living and looking at the ocean, playing in its waters and on the beach, and being in this house seemed to speak against everything that I thought living here was supposed to be about. I felt this down to my bones, but Damian was making it hard for me to not like him. Every time I tried to come up with something to say against the house, he just gave me a calm, rational answer that made him endearing.

Damian appeared just to my right, handing me a glass of nicely chilled white wine.

"Thanks," I said politely, taking a sip.

"See," Damian said as we looked out over the ocean, "we finished the tour, and the sun hasn't even set yet."

"You have a nice place here, Damian," I said to him. "I hope you make the most of it."

"Oh, I think I will," he told me as he took a sip of his drink. "I hope you like seafood," he said to me as he turned to walk inside.

I followed him into the house and walked over into the kitchen, where he had a big pot going on the stove already.

"Of course, I like seafood," I said to him, feeling slightly offended.

"Great," Damian answered as he took a small cooler out of the fridge and placed it on the counter next to the stove. "We have an indoor clambake tonight. I know it's probably not as good as what you're used to right on the beach, but at the last moment this is the best I could do."

I watched as Damian prepared everything, deftly taking the lobsters out of the cooler and placing them into the boiling water where the other items already were. He put the lid on the pot quickly to keep the lobsters from trying to work their way out. While the seafood boiled, I watched as he chopped items for a salad. He cut the greens and vegetables with great expertise and then made a quick vinaigrette with some olive oil, vinegar, garlic, and spices.

"I have to say I'm impressed," I told him.

"Impressed by what?" he asked as he tossed the salad lightly in a wooden bowl.

"I don't know, I guess I thought you would have a chef or wait staff or something taking care of all this for you," I told him. After I said it out loud, I realized how silly it sounded.

"I don't have a staff like that," he told me as he put the salad down on the table that was set for dinner. "James is my driver, and bodyguard, but that's all I have. Although I do have a cleaning service come in and clean my apartments and the house. I like to cook, so I try to do it myself. Hopefully, you'll appreciate it tonight."

I thought back to the notion that it might be the time for me to ask him about the road, the beach access, and what his house did to the area. Now seemed like a good time to have my say.

"You look like you want to ask me something," Damian said to me. He could see me watching him in the kitchen.

"Actually," I said, standing up straight on the other side of the counter where he was prepping food, "I do. You know, when you had this house built, they took away the public beach access to this area for everyone. It seems kind of selfish of you to do that, especially to people that really like this area of the beach. A lot of people love to come down to this end. The views are better, and it's off the boardwalk, so it doesn't get as crowded, but now they can't even walk down the street here."

I had gotten it all out and felt a little flush, unsure of what Damian was going to say in response. He put down the knife he was using and looked over at me, wiping his hands on a towel.

"Yeah, I felt bad about that," Damian said to me in a serious tone. "That wasn't my intent or even my idea. I knew the house was going to take up a lot of space, and the town insisted that I have the gate and the walls to keep things private. They decided it would be better if they just made the road private and closed off access. I wanted to put a pathway that led from the road around the house and out onto the beach, but the approval for that hasn't come through. They said maybe before next season, so I hope it goes through. I would like to let people onto the beach if they want to be there."

Once again, Damian had foiled my view of him by being Mr. Nice Guy. In fact, he was almost Mr. Too Nice Guy. There had to be something about him that wasn't so… perfect. I caught myself gazing at him as he bent over in the refrigerator to get something, and I blushed when he looked over his shoulder and saw me staring at him.

"Well, that would be very nice of you," I said softly, walking back towards the view out towards the water, sipping my wine.

"Shall we sit and have some salad while everything finishes?" Damian said to me as he came over to pull out the chair for me.

I sat down in the chair, and Damian gently pushed it closer to the table. He briefly placed his hands on my shoulders as he stood behind me, sending a chill through my body. He sat himself down in the chair across the table from me and passed me the salad, allowing me to take some first.

We sat and ate for a few minutes, with me picking lightly at my salad while I watched him from the corner of my eye. I couldn't help but notice that he was watching me the whole time until I finally put down my fork and looked directly at him.

"What?" I asked me abruptly.

"What are you talking about?" he asked in between bites of lettuce and cucumber.

"You keep looking at me like… well, like I don't know what, but you keep looking."

"I'm sorry," he said politely, wiping his mouth with his napkin and standing up from the table. He picked up his salad plate and put his hand out, waiting for me to hand him my dish. "I didn't mean to make you feel uncomfortable."

Damian placed the dishes in the sink and then began to place the clambake items on a large platter. He came back over to the table, placing the platter between us.

"I just find you very attractive," Damian said. He placed a lobster on my plate and handed me the serving utensils so I could help myself to corn, potatoes, clams, sausage or whatever else I might want. "I have since the first time I saw you in the bakery. I haven't been able to get you out of my head since then, and then when I saw you at the bar last night, I knew I just had to talk to you some more. So now I thought this might be a good chance to get to know you better."

I was a little taken aback by his statement. I wasn't surprised that he had an interest; hell, he had invited me over to his house. I guess I was caught off guard by the direct way that he said it to me. Most men I had come across were not nearly as bold to say how they felt. The ones I dealt with in town all were much meeker, had less confidence. Damian was nothing like that.

So, I went on to tell him more about myself as we ate dinner. He asked question after question, about what it was like to grow up in a small town in Delaware, what culinary school was like for me, why I left New York and came back home, starting the bakery, what my sisters were like, about my dog, and everything else in between. By the time we were finished with dinner, I felt exhausted from all the talking, even though I had managed to wolf down a whole lobster, a dozen clams, potatoes and more.

I sucked the last bit of meat from one of the lobster legs, slurping away as I did, and looked up at Damian as I did. He had a big smile on his face, almost as if he were in awe of what I was doing.

"Boy, you really make the most of eating a lobster," he commented.

"I suppose you just eat the tail and the claws," I told him as I looked over the pile of empty shells on my plate. "There's lots of great nooks and crannies you are missing when you do that you know. The lobster gave his life for our pleasure. The least we can do is make it last."

This brought about a hearty chuckle from Damian, the deepest I heard him laugh. He shook his head in disbelief at me as he cleared the platter of empty clam shells from the table. He came back over and started to clear away the rest of the plates.

"Let me help you," I said to him, picking up some items from the table and bringing them into the kitchen.

Damian was stacking dishes into the dishwasher, and I stood next to him, handing him item after item until everything was put inside. He closed the dishwasher door, latching it shut, and stood up quickly, bringing his body very close to mine. With him standing next to me like this, I could feel the electricity between us was strong. Damian was looking down into my eyes and slowly moved past me, his body brushing against mine as I leaned back against the counter. I inhaled a bit, my breath taken away from the experience.

He had walked back over to the table, picked up our wine glasses and poured us each another glass of white wine.

"Would you like to sit outside for a while?" Damian asked as he handed me my glass. "We can sit on the porch, or go down by the outdoor pool, or even out onto the beach if you like."

"Let's go out by the pool," I decided, wanting to see more of what it was like down there.

I started walking over towards the stairs, but instead, Damian walked over to the elevator door and pressed the button.

"We can take the elevator down," Damian said as the doors rattled open. "It will be easier to handle our wine glasses."

Damian held the door open for me so I could step inside first, and he followed and shut the outer door before closing the inner elevator door. The elevator was quite small, and you would have a hard time fitting a third person in there. As I felt it slowly move downward, I stood silently, looking down at my wine glass. I found it difficult to fight the strong attraction I felt. This wasn't like me, to find myself drawn to someone or even having a crush like this, but it was getting more difficult for me to deny.

The elevator seemed to move in slow motion, and when it finally settled on the second floor, we had to wait a moment for it to secure in place before the door would allow itself to open. There was a slight jolt, and I could feel myself losing my balance slightly. Damian braced me with his right hand, gently grabbing my elbow to hold me up before he opened the door. He then took my left hand in his right and helped me out of the elevator. His hand was strong and firm, stronger than I had expected of a guy who spends all day in an office. I couldn't help but notice that the palm of my hand was now noticeably sweaty.

Damian led me towards the pool, and we walked through the interior section and out a door that led to the back. The pool area outside was illuminated by solar lighting and casting from the bright moon that was now shining in the clear night sky. The temperature had cooled from the heat of the day, and there was a beautiful breeze blowing in off the ocean that we could feel as we took seats in lounge chairs positioned around the fire pit.

"Okay, I have to admit, I was skeptical of how nice this would look Damian, but it is beautiful out here." I took another sip of wine, having lost track of how much I had to drink so far tonight, and not really caring that much anymore.

"Thanks," he said to me with a laugh.

All we could hear is the combination of the ocean gently hitting the beach and the waterfall cascading down into the pool.

"You know," Damian said, breaking the silence, "after listening to you tonight, I think you and I have a lot in common."

I couldn't help but let out a hard laugh.

"Really?" I said in disbelief. "I don't know what you think we have in common. My house is about the size of your cabana back here, I drive a scooter, not a limo, and I work in a hot kitchen all day."

"That's all just cosmetic stuff, Kelly," Damian said to me seriously. "The house, the cars, all those things are nice to own, but they don't define me as a person. I'm a lot like you. I have two siblings, come from a strong family, own my own business, work hard, and take pride in what I do, and when I want something, I go after it."

"The difference is when you want something and go after it, you can afford to buy it."

"Money doesn't get you everything you want," Damian said as he sat back in his chair. He seemed a bit insulted by what I had said. "I put a strong effort into everything – my business, my family, and my relationships. It takes work, just like it does for you. Sure, having money gives me some advantages and perks, I don't deny that, and there are times where I use that to gain an edge. I'm using what I have at my disposal, and you would do the same thing. That's what a good businessperson does."

"I didn't mean that to come out as an insult, Damian," I said to him apologetically. "It's just a reality of the worlds we live in. You're right – if I had the money I am sure I would use it to my advantage at times too."

Damian got up from his chair and began to put some wood into the fire pit. He took a lighter from his pocket and lit the kindling, sparking the fire instantly. Within moments flames were licking up towards the sky. He then walked over to a large chest against the far wall and pulled out a green-checkered blanket and placed it at the foot of my lounge chair.

"In case you get chilly," he said to me.

"I'm actually feeling a little warm already," I said to him.

I stood up from the chair, kicked off my sneakers and pulled off my socks. I walked over towards the edge of the pool and sat down, dangling my feet into the water. The water was the perfect hint of cool I was looking for. I looked back over at Damian sitting in his chair, smiled, and then patted the ground, indicating that he should come over and sit next to me. He kicked off his shoes, grabbed our wine glasses, and came and sat down. Our arms were practically touching as I playfully moved my feet in the water.

"So, Damian," I said to him, finishing off what was left in my wine glass, "how is it that a rich, good-looking guy like you isn't already attached to someone?"

"You think I'm good-looking?" he said to me with a grin.

I pushed my shoulder up against him to give him a little shove.

"Are you going to answer me? You peppered me with questions all night."

"Fair enough," he said, emptying his wine glass. "I've spent so much of the past few years focusing on the work we do that I just haven't had time to devote to anyone, and, to be honest, I don't think I have met anyone in the past that I would want to be attached to."

I took notice of how he said "in the past" as he looked at me.

"But there must be all kinds of beautiful starlets and models that would love to go out with you," I asked him, brushing a stray hair from in front of my eyes.

"I don't know about that," he chuckled. "I've had dates with models and actresses, sure, but a lot of that stuff is set up by PR people so they can get good pictures for some magazine or website. I don't think I ever went out with someone like that more than once. I have less in common with them than I do with you."

I looked over at Damian and could see him staring deep into me. He slowly leaned down and kissed me, softly at first, but with greater strength as the kiss endured. I put my hand up to his cheek and held his lips to mine. We moved even closer to each other, our bodies pressing against one another as we balanced to avoid falling into the pool. Kiss after kiss lingered longer and longer until I could feel myself losing my breath and Damian slowly parted his lips from mine.

"That was nice," I said softly.

"I thought so too," he said in a hushed tone before leaning back in to kiss me again. Just as we started kissing more deeply, with Damian putting his arm around me, we heard the door open and close. I broke the kiss quickly and saw Damian look over as I turned to see who was there. It was James standing there.

"I'm sorry to interrupt you, boss," James said. "I didn't know you still had company. Good evening, Ms. Barton," he said politely.

"Hi, James," I said to him. I scrambled to my feet, the spell broken. "It's okay, I should get going anyway. It's getting late, and I've been up since four."

I walked back over and slipped my socks and sneakers back on my feet, and Damian followed me over to the chair.

"Are you sure you have to go?" I could see the disappointment on his face.

"I think I should," I told him.

"I can drive you home," Damian said. "You shouldn't walk home in the dark."

"No, it's fine. My scooter is back at the bakery. I can just walk over and get it. It's not a big deal."

"I'll drive you home," James said as he stepped up. "The Mustang is still in the driveway."

"Perfect," Damian said. "I'll walk you out, and James can meet us out there."

Damian looked over at James and nodded to him, and James nodded back.

"Just let me go grab the keys," James said, going back inside.

Damian walked me back into the house and then down the stairs towards the front door. We strolled out towards the driveway, where there was a red Mustang convertible parked. "Wow, nice car," I said to him, running my hand over the hood, feeling that it was still warm.

"It's one of my favorites," Damian said as he walked behind me. I stopped at the passenger side door and turned to look at him.

"Thank you for dinner," I told him. "I had a lovely time."

"It was my pleasure." Damian gave me another kiss. "Your sister said you were off tomorrow. Do you think you would like to get together? We can do whatever you would like, maybe spend some time at the beach, or in the pool, or out somewhere. Whatever you want to do. I want to see you again."

"I think we can do that," I answered with a smile. "Do you have your phone on you?"

Damian took out his phone, and I took it from his hand and put my phone number in his contacts.

"Call me in the morning and let me know what you want to do," I told him.

I leaned back into him and kissed him. Damian pressed my body up against the door of the car as he got closer to me. It was only the sound of James clearing his throat that made us break the kiss.

"All set?" James asked me as he walked around to the driver's side.

Damian opened the car door for me, and I slid into the passenger seat.

"See you tomorrow," Damian told me as he gave a light wave when we backed out of the driveway. I could see that he stayed in the driveway, watching to make sure we got off okay.

I sat back in the leather seat, giving James the short directions to get over to my house. I could feel the breeze blowing through my hair as we sped along the roads, and within moments we were pulling into my driveway.

"Thank you for the ride, James," I said to him as I climbed out, fishing my house keys out of my purse.

"You're welcome, Ms. Barton," James said to me.

"Please, call me Kelly," I told him.

"Okay, Kelly," he said with a laugh. "I guess I'll be seeing you tomorrow."

"Yes, you will." I walked up the path to my front door and unlocked the door, waving to James, who was waiting for me to get inside.

I noticed a sticky note placed just inside the door on the table where I normally put my keys. I picked up the note and saw it was from Jodie.

I came by and fed Alice for you. Hope the date went well. I want details!!
Call me!
J

Alice jogged out to greet me, and I bent down to pet her as she gave me a slobbering kiss. She followed me into my bedroom, where I sat on the bed and took off my shoes, socks, and jeans and just lay on the bed. Alice curled up next to me, getting ready to call it a night and glad that I was home. She was snoring almost immediately.

There was no way I was falling asleep that fast, not after the night I had.

11

Damian

The evening ended too soon when Kelly left. We were just starting to get closer when James and Shannon came home, and I was disappointed that she decided to leave right away. I went back inside after James left to take Kelly home and straightened up upstairs, putting things away before making myself another drink at the bar. I took my drink out onto the patio to overlook the ocean and enjoy the night breeze.

It wasn't long before Shannon showed her face, popping out onto the porch to join me. She sat down in one of the deck chairs and sat silently for a few moments before turning to me.

"Well, how was your night Shannon?" she said in a mock tone of my voice. "I had a lot of fun, Damian, thanks for asking."

"I'm sorry," I said, looking over to her. "I guess I was just lost in my thoughts. Did you and James have a good time?"

"Yes, in fact, we did," she said to me, sounding a little surprised. "I drove us up to Rehoboth, and we hit the outlets and did some shopping. Thanks for the new bathing suits and beachwear by the way. We then spent some time walking around, got some dinner, and picked out a few places that we might like to check out tomorrow if you're up for some fun. James is a pretty interesting guy. I didn't realize he had the past he has with the military and all. He's a badass."

"I'm glad you guys had fun, and thanks for running out on such short notice. As for your invitation for tomorrow, I'm spending the day with Kelly, so I'll have to beg off from whatever it is you guys are planning to do."

"So, I guess the date went well then if she is seeing you again right away?" Shannon asked me. "Bravo to you." Shannon toasted me with a beer she had grabbed from the fridge.

"It did go well, we had a nice time. Kelly is a wonderful woman – witty, gutsy, smart, fun to be with, and attractive. She has no problem putting someone in their place and standing up for herself. We had some great conversation."

"More than great conversation, from what I could see," James interjected as he walked out onto the porch with us, twisting open a beer bottle of his own and leaning against the railing to face Shannon and me.

"I guess you got Kelly home okay?" I asked, hoping to change the subject quickly before I had to hear it from Shannon.

"Home safe and sound, boss" James added before sipping his beer.

"What do you mean more than great conversation, James?" Shannon asked him. "Inquiring minds want to know."

"I don't want to speak out of turn here," James said coyly. "The boss signs my paychecks after all."

"You may as well tell her now, James," I said resignedly. "She's going to pester both of us until she gets the answer anyway."

"When I walked outside, they were sitting by the pool making out."

Shannon looked back and forth between James and me, her mouth open slightly.

"Wow, Damian, I'm impressed. I wish I had caught the show. And now you're seeing her again tomorrow? You must really like her. I can't remember the last time you saw a woman more than once, never mind two days in a row. Should I send out a press release?"

"You two are as bad as it would be having my brothers here right now," I answered them, shaking my head.

"I'm sure I can get them on a conference call right now if you want," Shannon said with a smile as she picked up her phone.

"Don't you dare," I told her firmly.

Shannon laughed as she started to lower her phone.

"I have a bunch of text messages from Paul, by the way, saying he needed to talk to you. He's tried calling you," Shannon added, taking a quick glance at her messages.

"I told Paul I didn't want to be bothered before we left. I don't care what it is he has to say; it can wait. I'm on vacation, and so are you. Put the phone away."

"What are you and Kelly going to do tomorrow?" Shannon asked. "Do you need me to help you plan anything?"

"Nope, this is all on me, Shannon. I'll make any arrangements of things to do. We may just spend time on the beach and at the house. I'll see what she wants to do in the morning and I'll pick her up, so you don't have to worry about it, James," I said to both.

"Can we take the Mustang again tomorrow?" Shannon asked with anticipation.

"Sure, I guess so. I'll take the truck," I answered.

"Awesome," Shannon said. "I can't wait to get behind the wheel again."

"No way," James said to her. "I'll be driving tomorrow. You were a little nuts behind the wheel. I can tell you live in the city from the way you drive. Leave it to the professionals."

"Fine," Shannon pouted.

Shannon finished off the last of her beer, shaking the empty bottle in her hand.

"Well, I'm empty," she said as she stood up and stretched. "How about a game of pool, Sarge, before I go to bed? I still want to try to kick your ass."

"Sarge?" I said, looking at her with surprise.

"Sarge," she said, pointing at James. "He was a sergeant in the army. I decided that's what I would call him now. You didn't know he was a sergeant?"

"I knew it," I told her, thinking back to when I first hired James and looked at his impressive military service record. "I'm just shocked he would tell you about it."

"You know how she is, boss," James replied. "She's relentless with asking questions. It was either give her some information or put up with her nagging me all night long. Besides, it was better than spending hours watching her pick out clothes."

"Never mind the stalling, Sarge," Shannon told him. "Let's go. You can play the winner if you want, Damian."

"No, I think I am going to sit here for a bit before I turn in," I told Shannon. "I have to think about what to do tomorrow with Kelly, and plan things out anyway."

"Well, if you change your mind about playing, or you need help with anything, come on down," Shannon told me.

"Besides, you would just end up playing me anyway, boss," James added as he walked towards the door to go back inside.

"Ugh, I want to beat you so bad now," Shannon said with disgust as she followed James indoors.

I was left alone on the porch, just listening to the ocean waves and the distant sounds of the few people out on the beach this late at night. I swirled the ice in my glass, listening to it click in rhythm as I looked up into the starry sky.

Shannon was right – I couldn't remember the last time I had seen a woman more than once or two days in a row. There hadn't been anyone that I had wanted to see again in a long time or anyone that had stirred me up as much as Kelly had in just a couple of days. Even I was feeling a little overwhelmed by it all.

I needed to make sure I came up with ways to make tomorrow fun for Kelly so that she would want to spend as much time as possible together. I set my brain in motion, going over different ideas of ways that I could romance her, and prove to her that I wasn't just some fat cat billionaire, but a strong man that knows how to make a woman feel special.

12

Kelly

I was always grateful for Monday mornings because it meant a little more sleep than usual, so I was more than a bit annoyed when I heard a knock at the door and saw it was only seven-thirty in the morning. Even Alice didn't have the energy to jump out of my bed to go see who was knocking, and I let the knocking continue until it got louder and more frantic.

I stormed out of bed, not even bothering to grab my robe to cover myself up and just answered the door wearing nothing by a white t-shirt and the black boyshort panties I had on. I threw the door open hastily, getting ready to yell at whoever I found on the other side. There was Jodie, grinning at me and holding two cups of coffee in her hands.

"Why are you here so early?" I complained. "I just want to sleep some more."

I marched myself over to my couch and plopped down on it, laying my face on the nearest throw pillow.

"I wanted to see how your date went yesterday," Jodie answered.

I didn't say anything and continued to just lay on the couch, hoping she might just leave so I could get another hour of sleep in.

"Can I do more than look at your ass while I'm here?" Jodie yelled. "Roll over and talk to me, Kelly! I want to know how it went."

I exhaled deeply and flipped myself over, keeping an arm over my eyes in the hopes of blocking the sunlight out of them.

"We had dinner and talked and had a very nice time," I told her. "Can you leave now?"

"Really? That's all you're going to say about it? You had a nice time? Come on, Kelly, you were gone long enough where I had to come over and let Alice out and feed her, and you didn't answer any texts or anything. I don't even know what time you got home. And your scooter is still locked up at the boardwalk."

"Shit, I forgot about the scooter. Did you bring it?" I asked.

"No, I didn't bring it. I don't have the combination to your lock. But if you give me the combination, and some details, I will gladly go get it for you."

I sat up on the couch and looked over at Jodie through my peering, barely-open eyes. She held out the travel cup of coffee for me, and I grabbed it, taking a slow sip at first to see how hot it was. I could tell right away it was something she made at home and not something she got from the Wah Wah down the street. I felt the slow jolt from the coffee perk me up a bit and looked up at Jodie.

"38-32-12," I said to her, giving her the combination. "The keys are by the door. Bring my scooter back, and I'll gladly give you details."

"Back in ten minutes," Jodie said as she hopped out of the chair. "Put some shorts on at least in case someone else comes to the door," she said with a laugh. I sneered back at her and sat drinking my coffee as she walked out the door.

Jodie was back in under ten minutes, during which time I did throw a pair of Terry shorts on and let Alice out in the back. I sat myself down at the small table on the patio while Alice sniffed around the yard. I heard the wooden gate to the backyard open and close as Jodie came back and sat with me.

"Scooter is delivered," she said, dropping the keys on the table. "So, let's have it. Start at the beginning."

I slowly went over the details of my evening with Damian, lingering over the details of the house so that Jodie could soak in just how the place looked and how decadent it all seemed. After telling her about each floor, the giant kitchen, and the amazing view, I told her how I tried to make my points to him, and how Damian used his charm, good manners, and personality to refute everything from me perfectly. I talked about the lovely dinner, how he cooked, and we drank and talked and about how idyllic the evening was.

"And that's it? You ate dinner and came home?" Jodie said in disbelief. "I'm not buying it."

I pulled my knees up, so they were close to my body and sipped my coffee. I could just barely see Jodie's face over my kneecaps as I talked.

"Okay, so there was a little more. We might have made out for a little while, down by the pool," I said quickly.

Jodie bolted up in her seat so she could see my face smiling back at her. She smacked my knee playfully.

"What the hell, Kelly? Why did you wait so long to mention that?"

"It happened right at the end of the night," I told her. "We were talking, and having wine, and the mood was right, and he just leaned in and started kissing me. Before I knew it, we just kept at it."

"So how was it? Never mind, I can tell already it was amazing with the way you are blushing."

"It was amazing," I admitted. "His lips were… well, they were perfect. The best kisses I have had in many years."

"Then what happened?" Jodie asked, anticipating much more.

"Nothing," I told her. "James showed up and interrupted our kissing, and that was it. I said I needed to leave, Damian walked me to the car, we kissed some more, and James drove me home."

"Well, that's disappointing."

"No, it was very nice," I said to her. "Damian is going to call me this morning so we can go out today."

"Where are you going to go? What will you do? Do you think he'll take you somewhere fancy? Maybe you can helicopter out to his yacht or ride up to Dover and take his private plane somewhere," Jodie said, fantasizing about what might happen.

"What makes you think he has a helicopter, yacht and private plane around here?"

"Come on, Kelly, the guy's a billionaire. Of course, he has that stuff." Jodie looked at me like I was crazy for thinking otherwise.

"I think you've read too many romance books," I said rolling my eyes at her.

"What, do you think he's just going to want to go over to Ocean City, play mini golf and get some fried clams? I'm sure he expects more than that."

"You don't know Damian at all, Jodie. You talked to him for two minutes in the bar. I spent hours with him last night. He's nothing like what you think he is. He's not hung up on how much money he has or anything like that. He's a regular guy who is nice, and funny, and caring…"

"And has a mansion, expensive toys and more money in his wallet than I have in the bank," Jodie added. "That's not a regular guy, Kelly. He may come across that way to you, but he's not regular. We're regular."

I stood up from my chair and looked down at Jodie.

"You're starting to piss me off," I said to her as I walked back inside the house.

"Why?" she yelled after me as she followed me in.

I sat down at the kitchen table and grabbed a banana from the bowl in front of me, quickly peeling it and taking a bite.

"Because you're making assumptions about him based on how much money he has, and you're doing the same thing about us. Just because we earn different amounts of money doesn't mean we're so different, or that he's better than us or even thinks he is better than us. Damian and I have a lot in common, I think, and I don't think he has expectations of me because I don't have a lot of money in the bank."

"Okay, you're right, "Jodie admitted. "I'm sorry. I didn't mean for it to come out that way. I guess I'm just excited for you, and maybe a little jealous, that he's interested in you. Stuff like that doesn't happen to people around here every day, you know."

I could hear my cell phone ringing off in the distance. Jodie and I looked at each other, and I jumped up from the table, stubbing my foot on the chair she was sitting on along the way. I hopped and hobbled down the hallway, rushing to get to the phone before it stopped ringing. I grabbed the phone and pressed answer, sitting down on the bed to rub my aching toes.

"Hello?" I asked.

"Kelly?" the voice on the other end asked. "Hi, it's Damian. I hope it's not too early to call and I didn't wake you."

Jodie appeared in the doorway to look at me.

"No, it's not too early," I told Damian. "I was up already." I shot Jodie a glare as I said this.

"Oh, good. I was just wondering if you might like to get together this morning. I could swing by and pick you up in a few minutes, and we could plan out our day."

A sense of panic came over me as I looked at the time on my phone and saw it was 8:15.

"Well, I'm not quite ready to start the day just yet," I told him, trying to buy myself some time. "Do you think you could pick me up around nine instead?"

"Sure thing," Damian said. "I'll see you at nine. What's your address?"
"It's 14 Sapphire Pointe. I'll see you in a bit." I hung up the phone and tossed it onto the bed.

"He's going to be here in 45 minutes," I said to Jodie, suddenly feeling panicked. "I need to shower, and get something to wear for the day, pack a bag in case we go to the beach, take care of Alice…"

"Kelly, relax," Jodie said as she came up and put her hands on my shoulders. "I will take Alice for the day. Go take your shower, and I'll pack a bag for you. You have plenty of time."

"Okay thanks," I said to Jodie as I went into the bathroom and turned the shower on. I stripped off my clothes, tossing them in the hamper, and the peeked my head out the bathroom back into the bedroom to see Jodie going through my closet. "Jodie," I said to her seriously, "Be nice about what you pack, okay?"

"I don't think you have anything to worry about it," Jodie said to me as she flipped hanger after hanger of clothing. "There's nothing but nice in here anyway."

I closed the bathroom door, and the room immediately started getting steamy from the shower. I tried to work my way through the shower as quickly as I could, knowing I didn't have a lot of time before Damian was knocking on the door. I wanted to be sure I had time to dry my hair at least before he got here.

Once I got out of the shower, I wrapped a towel around myself and open the door, letting the steam spew out into the bedroom. I saw Jodie packing some things into a bag for me, and she turned and looked at me standing in the doorway.

"That was fast," she commented as she looked at my choice of shoes and tossed a pair of heels into my bag.

"I'm never going to wear those," I said to her, walking over and pulling the heels out of the bag.

"Why not?" Jodie asked. "They'll make you a little taller, so he doesn't have to bend so far to kiss you." Jodie grinned at me as I tossed the heels back into my closet.

"I'll wear my sandals," I told her. "Besides, Damian had no problem kissing me last night," I told her as I tossed my hair back and went back into the bathroom.

I pulled out my hair dryer and went through the routine of drying my hair, something I rarely did these days, mainly because I just didn't have time to do it. I brushed my hair out as I dried it, giving it some nice waves and a little bit of curl that cascaded around my shoulders.

I bounded out of the bathroom again and saw Jodie sitting on my bed, looking at her phone. She took a quick look at me, giving me the once-over.

"Let me do your toenails," Jodie said to me, pointing for me to sit on the bed.

"Jodie, I never do my nails. It's not worth it."

"I'm not talking about your fingernails. The way we work, I wouldn't waste my time. But you can at least have nice-looking toes if you're wearing sandals all day." Jodie walked over and grabbed a nail kit and nail polish off my dresser.

"Fine," I sighed, "but make it fast. I still need to get dressed, and Damian's going to be here in like twenty minutes."
"If you stop fidgeting around, I can get started." Jodie grabbed my feet and pulled them up onto her lap.

"Remember when we used to do this when we were in high school?" Jodie said as she sculpted my toenails and got them ready for painting. I giggled a little as she gripped the sensitive sole of my left foot.

"I do," I told her. "You were always helping me get ready for dates. You know I was never good at this stuff. Thank God I had you around; I don't think I would have ever gotten any second dates without your help. I was the older sister and should have been the one helping you."

Jodie was deftly putting a coat of nail polish on my toes.

"You did help me," Jodie said to me. "Just in different ways. I would never have made it through school without your help. And remember who the one was crying to you on the phone when you were in New York, and I was back here, trying to find my way and what to do with my life? If it hadn't been for you, I probably would have run off with Ben and gone out to Oregon. Who knows what would have happened then. Then you came back here, and you gave me some direction and a career. I don't know if I have ever told you this, but I am so grateful for all you have done for me. I couldn't ask for a better big sister."

"Don't get me all misty-eyed, Jodie," I said to her as I choked up. "I have a date coming in about five minutes."

"Sorry," she replied, wiping her own eyes and laughing. "Your toes are done. You better get dressed." Jodie handed me some clothes, and I saw she had given me a thin-strapped yellow dress.

"Jodie, I'm not wearing a dress," I said to her, handing it back to her. I walked over to my dresser and pulled out a pair of white shorts and a purple tank top to wear instead.

"What's wrong with the dress?" she asked me as she held it up. I had already put on my panties and was just fastening my bra as quickly as I could.

"There's nothing wrong with it, I just don't want to wear a dress all day and worry about it flying up if we're walking on the beach. Not to mention that I don't want to flash all the teenage boys that hang out under the boardwalk hoping to look up skirts. I'm wearing shorts."

"Okay," Jodie said in a huff, "but I am packing this dress for you in case you want something to wear tonight." Jodie stuffed the dress into my bag and closed it up. Just as she finished, I heard a knock on the door.

"Shit, he's here already," I said as I zipped up my shorts. "Jodie, get the door please so I can finish getting dressed. And be nice to him. No prying."

"Yeah, yeah," she said, waving her hand at me. I knew she wasn't going to pay attention to what I said as she closed my bedroom door.

I snatched up my tank top and put it on, adjusting the straps, and then I slipped into my sandals. I glanced at my reflection in the mirror and was happy with what I saw. I looked like I wanted to: no makeup, no fancy hairstyle, just me.

This is how I want him to like me, I thought to myself as I smiled.

I picked up my sunglasses from my dresser, grabbed my keys and purse and the bag Jodie had packed, took a deep breath, and opened the bedroom door. I walked down the short hall into the living room, where I saw Damian sitting on the couch, with Jodie sitting in the chair across from him, and Alice firmly planted in front of Damian as he scratched her head and her tail wagged happily.

"So how many limos do you own?" I heard Jodie ask as I came closer.

Damian stood up as I stood next to Jodie, bumping her chair with my hip to get her to keep quiet. I could see Damian looking at the bag I was carrying.

"I packed a few things because I wasn't sure what we were doing today," I said, hoping to temper any expectations he might have about how the day or night might go. "I hope that's okay."

"That's perfect," Damian said to me. I felt his eyes scanning over me, looking at my less-than-tan legs in my shorts. His gaze worked its way up to meet mine, and we stood staring at each other for a moment.

"Well, I guess I'll take Alice and go," Jodie said, breaking the spell between us. She stood up and grabbed Alice's leash, and

Alice rushed over to her, bouncing up and down, knowing she was going out or in the car.

"You two have a great time today," Jodie told us. "Call me or text me and let me know when you want Alice back, Kelly." Jodie shot a big grin while she looked at Damian from behind him, taking notice of his strong legs in his own pair of shorts.

"Shall we go?" Damian asked me, offering to take my bag for me.

I nodded and handed him the small duffle bag as he led the way out the front door. I saw a big white pick-up truck in the driveway waiting for us.

"No Mustang today?" I asked Damian as we got to the truck.

"No, I told James he could use it today. I thought the truck might be good for us."

Damian opened the passenger door for me so I could climb in, and I had to climb, bracing myself on the door frame with my right hand while Damian held my left to help me get a boost up.

"I think I need a ladder to get in and out of this thing," I said, looking over my shoulder at Damian. I could see that he had taken a quick peek at my backside as I was getting in, and he looked a little sheepish that I had seen him looking, but I said nothing about it and just enjoyed it.

Damian came around to the driver's side and got in and started up the truck with a roar. He backed out of the driveway, and I glanced out the window and felt like we were towering over anything and everything outside.

"Ready to start our adventure for the day?" Damian asked me, smiling at me.

"You bet," I answered, smiling back. I wondered just what the day was going to hold for us, and the butterflies in my stomach started to ease a bit as Damian slid his hand over and took mine in his as he started to drive.

13

Kelly

The morning was already quite warm, and I was grateful for the cool air conditioning in Damian's truck as he started down the street. I looked over at him as he drove and I could see the signs of some stubble on his face, giving him a rugged look I had not noticed in him before that made my stomach flutter a bit more. It was only after I was staring at him for a moment that I noticed we were stopped at a stop sign and he was asking me a question.

"What was that?" I said, breaking the spell that was on me.

"I said do you want to grab some breakfast first before we start out for the day?" Damian smiled at me, almost as if he was taking pride in the fact that I was staring at him.

"Sure, that would be great." I regained my composure and turned my eyes straight ahead.

"Any recommendations about where to go?" he asked. "This is your town, you would know the best places to go."

"I know just the spot," I said to him with a smile.

I directed Damian over to where we could park and walk to the boardwalk and go to the Turtle Beach Café, my favorite spot for breakfast at the beach. Not that I got to go there much anymore since I was always at the bakery at breakfast time, but Turtle Beach was always a place I enjoyed in my younger days. Jodie and I went here often when we were teens during the summer, or after we went to church on Sundays and wanted to get out of the house for a bit.

Damian and I walked up to the café and entered. There was a crowd, just as there always was, but it was a bit less on Mondays, making it a little easier for us to get one of the tables and sit down.

"Are you sure this is where you want to go?" Damian said as he looked around. "You're at the boardwalk every day. Maybe you want something a little…"

"A little nicer?" I said to him, staring back at him. "This place has been here for years, Damian. It's a beach landmark, the people are great, and the food is awesome. Not everything has to be served on fine china with fancy silver and cost fifty dollars you know."

"I'm sorry," he said to me. "I didn't mean for it to come out that way. I just… I just want to make sure we have a nice day. If this is what you want, then it is perfect for me."

After the waitress came over and took our orders for coffee, I put the menu down and looked over at Damian. I could see he was struggling to find something he might want to try. I reached over, pulled the menu from his hands, and put it on top of mine.

"How about this," I stated. "We each get to choose different things we do today. It will give us a chance to get to know each other a little better and maybe try some new things. We'll start with me choosing breakfast for us, and then you get the next choice."

Damian seemed a little reluctant to go along with me, and I could see some concern on his face.

"Well I did make some plans for things to do today," he told me.

"I'm sure it's nothing we can't change or cancel if we have to. Besides, if you're planning to spend time living down here, don't you want to know about the area you're living in? Who better to show you around than someone local? Trust me, it will be a good day."

"Fair enough," he told me as the waitress arrived with our coffees.

"What can I get you?" the young waitress said, turning to me with a smile.

"We'll both have the breakfast panini, bacon, egg, and cheese," I said to her, handing her the menus.

Damian looked at me as he sipped his coffee. I think he was both taken by surprise that I was willing to take some control of the situation and impressed that I would say what was on mind.

"So," I started, "I told you all about me last night. Let's hear a little about more about you. Besides knowing that you own a big company, have a big house, lots of cars and a driver, I don't really know much about you. I mean, I guess I could have Googled you, but I would rather hear it from you."

"Okay." Damian put his mug down and looked straight at me. His eyes felt like they were penetrating mine as he told me about his family, his brothers, and his life as the son of a congressman. He talked about how hard it was after his mother passed away when he was a teenager, and what life was like for him growing up.

"What made you want to start a business like yours?" I asked him.

"I've always loved the ocean, ever since I was little and we would go out on the boat with my father. I thought about becoming an oceanographer first, but I decided I could have an even stronger impact if I had a business that focused on helping to clean up the ocean waters, making things better for everyone globally and not just in my backyard. So, I went to work coming up with ideas, and when we came up with a system that would help reduce the plastic in the waters to get rid of the pollution, it was a real breakthrough. Once countries saw it could work, they started taking the issue to heart, and I was able to grow the company. We've come up with some great methods that can help get rid of the garbage islands in the Pacific, and we're working on water bottles that are completely biodegradable and not made of plastic, which will be a big step towards eliminating trash in the oceans and in landfills. I feel like I'm really making a difference, and it's fun to go to work each day feeling that way."

"Wow, your family must be really proud of you," I replied.

"I think they are, though I have butted heads more than once with my father as he does his work with the government. My brother Chris is a lawyer whose clients I have fought with a few times as well, so it makes for some spirited conversations at holiday dinners. Other than that, I think they are glad about what I have been able to accomplish."

The waitress arrived and placed the plates down in front of us. Damian looked down at his sandwich, nicely toasted with layers of perfectly cooked egg, crisp bacon, and melted cheese. He watched me as I picked up a sandwich half and dove right into it, making a loud crunch. He followed suit, biting into his sandwich and leaving a long trail of cheese pulling from the sandwich and eventually clinging to his chin. After that first bite, Damian ate his sandwich with greater vigor as he realized just how tasty it was. Before we knew it, we had both polished off our breakfasts.

I glanced up at Damian and saw him licking the crumbs off his fingers and laughed out loud. I think he felt a little embarrassed at first, but within moments he went right back to finish what he was doing.

"That sandwich was awesome," he said, taking the last bit off his index finger.

"See, I told you to trust me." I reached to pick up the check the waitress had left on the table, but Damian snatched it up before I could get it.

"There's no way I'm letting you pay for this," he said to me, taking the check in his hand.

"Why not?" I said to him. "It was my idea to come here."

"I was the one who asked you out for the day. I should be taking care of you." Damian stood up from the table, took a ten out of his wallet, and left in on the table as a tip.

"I'll let you take it this time, Damian," I told him. "But you should know that I don't expect you to pay my way, even if you did ask me out. I can take care of myself."

"Oh, I don't doubt that for a minute, Kelly, not for one minute."

Damian paid our check, and we began a leisurely walk along the boardwalk back towards where we parked the car. There were a lot more people out and about now, and the sun was beating down on us as we moved along. Even though we had just stepped outside, I could see that Damian was already starting to perspire a little.

"It's a lot hotter out than I thought it might be," he said as he wiped his brow with the back of his hand.

"August at the beach," I said to him casually as we walked along. "Once September rolls around it will be a lot more comfortable. You'll enjoy it more. It's still sunny and nice, the ocean water is warm, and there are a lot fewer visitors around here."

"That's not great for your business," Damian remarked.

"No, business slows down a lot once the summer ends, but we still manage to do well throughout the year. We cut back our hours some, close on Mondays and Tuesdays, don't make quite as much of a variety of things to save money, things like that. I also do more cake decorating then to supplement the business. It's worked out pretty well for us so far."

"Sounds like you have things pretty well covered," he said as we reached the staircase to lead us off the boardwalk.

Damian took my hand as we walked down the wooden steps, looking back to make sure I made it down okay. When we got to the bottom of the steps, he kept holding my hand as we walked along to the car.

"Now what?" I asked him as he opened the door for me and boosted me up so I could get in the truck. Damian walked around to the driver's side and let himself in, starting up the truck.

"Now it's my turn to do something," he said as he looked at his watch. "I think we have plenty of time still to get there." "Get where?" Now I was curious as to what he had planned.

"You'll just have to wait and see," he told me as he hit some buttons on his phone to pull up the GPS to guide him where we were going. "Just sit back and relax for a little bit," he told me.

I watched out the window as the truck made its way north up Route 1 for a while, before heading west to 14 and crossing into Maryland.

"Damian, where are we going?" I asked as we kept heading west.

"It's not much longer. We'll be there soon."

Not much longer turned out to be almost another hour as we reached the Eastern Bay area. I was watching keenly out the window, hoping for some clue to see where we were going when I saw Damian turn left and start heading towards a large clearing. As we came up over the hill, I saw looming before us a hot air balloon. The balloon was a rainbow of colors and looking at it against the clear blue sky made the color formation pop even more to me like it was right off a calendar page.

Damian parked the truck on the grass about fifty yards away from the balloon, right next to a couple of other pickups in the area. Damian got out of the truck and walked over to my side, opening the door for me.

"We're here," he said with a smile, offering his hand to me to help me out.

I kept staring at the immense balloon over in the clearing and finally looked at Damian once I was on the ground. He was walking over to the back of the truck, grabbing a small knapsack and slinging it over his shoulder before walking back over to me.

"You mean we're getting in that?" I said to him, still with the stunned look on my face.

"Sure, I thought it would be fun. They're going to take us over the Eastern Shore and the Chesapeake Bay. It will be beautiful. Have you ever been in a balloon before?"

I gripped Damian's arm tightly as he started to walk towards the balloon, bringing him to a halt.

"Damian, "I said quietly, "I've never even been on an airplane, never mind a balloon."

"What are you talking about?" he questioned as if he didn't believe me. "You lived in New York for a few years, you must have been on an airplane to get there or to travel."

"I always drove to New York or Delaware when I went back and forth, and I've never traveled anywhere that I couldn't drive to. I've never been west of West Virginia." I was sure Damian could hear the tremble in my voice as I began to get more fearful with every stride we took that brought us closer to the balloon.

"Trust me, it's perfectly safe," Damian said, trying to reassure me as we got within about twenty feet of the balloon.

An older gentleman strode over to us, wearing a t-shirt and blue jeans, and firmly shook Damian's hand. He introduced himself as Todd, owner of the company, and said he would be taking us up today as soon as we were ready.

"Damian, I don't know if I can do this." I felt more and more intimidated every time I looked at the immense balloon.

"Miss, you have nothing to worry about," Todd told me calmly. "I've been flying for over twenty years, I've gone on thousands of flights, and I've never had a problem. The basket is nice and stable and comfortable, we only go up about a thousand feet or so, and I'll be taking care of everything to make sure it is enjoyable for you."

Only a thousand feet? Does this guy realize just how high that is? My inner voice was doing everything it could to convince me that this was a bad idea.

Damian turned to me and looked into my eyes. "Kelly, if you don't want to do this, just say so. It won't hurt my feelings if you're scared to try it."

As soon as Damian said the word "scared," I started to get my back up and felt a surge of bravery move through me.

"I'm not scared," I said defiantly. I stood up straight and looked at Todd. "Let's go," I stated calmly and started moving towards the balloon. I looked back as I reached the basket and I could see Damian chuckling to himself as he followed me.

Todd got us both settled into the basket. It was a lot more challenging to get into the basket than I ever thought it would be, and Damian gave me a helpful boost so I could bring myself aboard. The sides of the wicker basket were higher than I had imagined, and the basket seemed much stronger than what I had always envisioned when you see them on TV or in the movies. I even stamped my feet on the floor before takeoff just to see what it was like.

Todd could see I had some panic on my face as he and his crew were readying everything for us to take off.

"If you think you have a fear of heights, this is the perfect way for you to challenge that," he told me. "The ride is much more stable than you think it will be, and we move with the wind, so it is very smooth for passengers. I want the ride to be enjoyable for you, so you just let me know if you have any questions or concerns."

I did feel a little bit better, and Damian took my hand in his as soon as Todd fired up the propane burners to pump more hot air into the balloon so we could take off. I felt the lift start beneath us as the crew untied the balloon. Part of me wanted to bury my face into Damian's chest as we ascended, but I wanted him to see I could overcome any fear and I turned to look as we started going up.

I could see the crew beneath us gradually get smaller as we climbed the sky and started to move along with the wind. I had worried about just how fast we would get moving, but Todd let us know the balloon rarely went beyond six or eight miles per hour.

"How… how far are we going to travel?" I croaked.

"It's hard to say," Todd answered as he looked at me. "We go as far as the wind will let us. We're scheduled to fly for about an hour so it will be several miles, at least. Just relax and enjoy the view." Todd pointed out towards the east, and I got a clear view of the coastline beneath us. Seeing the water and the shore from this view was truly breathtaking, and I moved closer to the edge of the basket so I saw out more clearly.

Damian must have sensed that I was getting more comfortable with my surroundings, and he stood next to me, putting an arm around my waist.

"What do you think?" he said as we looked out and saw the amazing views, the birds flying by, and even a few boats out in the water as we quietly soared through the area.

"It is beautiful," I said to him as I gazed outward.

I went to take my phone out of my pocket to take some pictures and snapped off a couple as we went along.

"You don't have to do that," Damian told me. "There's a photographer with the chase crew that will meet us when we land. He's taking pictures of everything for us. We can just enjoy the view as we see it. It's much nicer that way."

We cruised along for quite a while, with Todd pointing out things for us to look at and watch. We were down low enough to skirt some treetops, which was a little intimidating, and Damian reached out and snagged a few leaves from one of them to present to me. At one point, we saw a few dolphins playing in the water off the coast. We even had kids wave to us from the beach as we went by.

The whole experience was much more exhilarating than ever imagined it could be, and by the time we were coming to an end and starting our descent, I was feeling disappointed that it was over. Todd guided the balloon gently down into an open field, and the chase crew was there to greet us to wrangle the balloon. We posed for a couple of pictures inside the basket and then celebrated with a champagne toast to our flight. I even received a certificate to mark my official first flight in a balloon.

The chase crew took us back to where our vehicle was located, and I still had a bit of a rush from the experience. I sat in the truck next to Damian as we headed out and back towards Bethany Beach, gazing out the window and at the sky and the view.

"Did you enjoy it?" Damian asked me as we drove along.

"It was incredible, Damian," I told him. "Thank you so much for that. That was something I can honestly say I never would have done on my own."

"Great," he said, beaming back at me. I could see he glanced at the clock on the dashboard before turning his eyes back to the road.

"We probably won't get back to Bethany until about four," Damian added. "Maybe we can go grab an early dinner, and since I picked the balloon ride, that means the next stop is your choice."

I knew immediately just where we should go, and I gave Damian directions, taking us back towards Bethany Beach and then out towards Ocean City. It was about four o'clock when I directed Damian to turn right into the parking lot, and we were lucky enough to find a spot easily.

"What's this place?" Damian said, hopping out of the car and looking around.

"It's Seacrets," I told him. I grabbed my bag from the back of the truck to take it in with me. I could already get the salty smell of the ocean air mixing with whatever Caribbean grilled foods they had going on inside. "Did you bring a bathing suit?"

Damian looked at me like I was crazy. "I thought we were just getting an early dinner and some drinks. Why do I need a bathing suit?"

"Trust me, you need one," I told him. Damian shrugged and then grabbed his bag from the truck, taking it with him.

I directed Damian over to the changing station located in the parking lot between the front entrance and the end of the street so we could change into our suits. I was hoping Jodie had been kind and packed a practical bathing suit for me, and lucky enough she had put two in there. One was a black bikini with a halter top, and the other was a simple sage green one-piece suit with a scoop neck to give me a little modesty. I decided on the one-piece and slid into it, tugging it in all the right places to get the best look. I slipped my sandals back on, took my towel from the bag, and walked out to see Damian was there waiting for me.

He was wearing a classic pair of red swim trunks and sandals, and it was now that I could get a better look at his body. He was more sculpted than the clothing I had seen him in let on. He clearly worked out a lot and had the ripped abs and strong pecs you expect to see on an athlete. Excitement raced in my body a bit from the way he looked and the way he was looking at me in my bathing suit.

"All set?" I asked him, trying not to let my voice quiver as I watched him.

"Sure, let's go," he replied.

We walked through the front entrance and made our way through some of the crowd indoors towards the outside where there was a beach bar. Damian started to walk towards the round tables located just beyond the bar under some palm trees, but I kept walking further. I turned and waved to him to follow me.

"What's out here?" he asked, but he soon saw where I was going as we appeared on the beach. People were sitting in the sand and at some tables on the beach, but there were also tables out in the calf-deep water that you could sit on. Beyond the tables were inflatables where you could lounge in the water.

One of the staff members walked up to us, and I asked her if Susan was working today. Susan and I went way back, having gone to high school together, and I knew she was one of the managers here that might be able to help me. I had helped her out many times with pastries and cakes for parties held at the bar and restaurant, and she always told me to ask for her if I came out here, but I never really had occasion to until now.

Glancing at Damian, I could see him taking in the amazing view. The sky was still crystal clear, and there were some boats and jetskis making their way across the water just beyond the inflatables area.

Susan quickly appeared at my side and gave me a hug.

"You finally came out here!" she exclaimed.

"Yeah, Monday is my day off, and I thought this would be a great place to bring a friend," I answered. Tugging on Damian, I pulled him over towards me.

"Susan Howard, this is Damian Woods. Damian, Susan is an old friend of mine and one of the managers here."

"Nice to meet you," Damian said, speaking loud enough to get his voice over the reggae music currently blaring from the outdoor sound system.
I could see Susan look Damian up and down, shaking his hand politely when she did. She turned to me and gave me a big smile, indicating her approval of the way Damian looked.

"What can I do for you, Kel?" she asked me.

"Do you have any floats still open we could use?"

I could see Susan scan the water and then look at the clipboard she had in her hand.

"I've got one out there on the left," she pointed. "It's all yours. Enjoy."

"Thanks," told her, leaning in to give her another hug.

"I want the whole story on where you snagged him from," Susan whispered to me.

"I'll call you during the week," I said as we broke our hug.

Damian and I began to make our way out to the blue and white inflatable, working through the warm ocean water. I didn't get much time to spend in the water anymore, and the reminder of the ocean floor squishing between my toes made me smile.

We reached the inflatable, and I worked to pull myself in, grabbing one of the handles for support. I felt Damian put his hand on my thigh to help me get my leg up and over, and I felt chills run up my body just from his touch. Once I was in and settled, Damian got right in easily, using his strong arms and legs. We settled into one side so that we could easily look out over the water by turning to the left or see the beach and the bar by turning to the right.

"This place looks great," Damian remarked as he scanned the crowd. "But I should have got us a couple of drinks before we came out here."

"Not a problem." I pointed to a young man working his way out to our raft with a tray in his hand. He was well-bronzed from spending the summer in the sun and gave us a welcoming smile.

Hey guys, I'm Chris," he told us, spinning his empty tray on his left index finger as he talked to us. "Welcome to Seacrets. Can I get you something to drink?"

"I'll have a Dirty Banana," I spoke up.

"A Red Stripe for me," Damian stated.

"Perfect," Chris told us. "Be back in a minute." Chris waded his way back to shore to put in our drink order as Damian looked at me through his sunglasses.

"What?" I asked him.

"A Dirty Banana? Sounds kind of… well, dirty." He smiled at me and waited for my response.

I could feel my cheeks blush a bit.

"It's really good. It's banana and coffee liqueurs, and cream, and fresh bananas. A perfect tropical taste." I was trying to cover up my hint of embarrassment.

The gentle sway of the raft in the water, combined with the warmth of the sun, even at this hour of the day, made the setting perfect. I laid my head back on the edge, feeling the tip of my ponytail just brush the top of the warm water, and I could feel myself move my head slightly back and forth, running my hair over the top of the water just like I used to do when I was a child out on a raft in the water.

Chris arrived shortly with our drinks, and that first slurp of my frosty drink through the straw gave me a blast of banana flavor. I could see Damian watching me as I took a long sip to watch my reaction.

"Did you want a taste?" I offered, pointing the straw towards him.

"Are you asking me to have a taste of your dirty banana?"

I laughed strongly when I heard him say this.

"I guess I am," I said boldly.

"I'll pass this time and stick to my beer," he said, holding up the sweating beer bottle.

"Your loss," I said to him coyly.

We lounged on our raft for a while, finished our drinks, and then each had one more. By the time we were each into our second drink, I had moved closer to Damian, resting my head on the arm he had placed around me.

"How about we get something to eat?" Damian suggested.

"Sure. We can get changed and then grab a table outside or inside, whatever you want."

"Let's eat out here. I love the atmosphere," Damian said.

He rolled himself out of the raft and then held his arms out to help me do the same. I slid over the side, and he caught me around the waist, letting his hands linger there for a moment before taking my hand in his and leading me out of the water. He caught up to our waiter, Chris, to pay the tab, but Chris let him know that Susan had taken care of the bill.

Now I really have to make sure to fill her in, I thought to myself.

Damian and I both walked off to our respective changing rooms to get out of our wet suits and dressed for dinner. I opened my locker, took my bag out and peeled out of my damp bathing suit. I saw the dress that Jodie had tucked into the bag, rolling it up nicely so that it had just the slightest of wrinkles. I slipped the yellow dress over my head and shimmied into it. The dress clung lightly to my damp body, but I liked the way it looked, and it made me feel more feminine than what I usually took the time to wear.

By the time I got out of the changing station, Damian was standing there waiting for me, wearing khaki shorts and a short sleeve button down shirt to go with his sandals. I watched him as his eyes locked onto me as I moved toward him, never

breaking away. I took this as a good sign of him liking the way
I looked.

Damian reached and took my bag for me as we walked them
back to the truck.

"You look great," he said as he slammed the truck door closed.

"Thanks." I tossed my damp hair back a bit, feeling it curling
from the water and the humidity.

We got back towards the outdoor dining area, and Susan
greeted us there and seated us at a nice table out of the direct
sun but also within view of the band that was set up. I took a
glance over and saw the familiar shape of the lead singer and
knew right away it was Captain Caraway and the Seeded Ryes.
Within moments the band started playing, breaking into
"Kokomo," always a beach favorite. Damian looked over at
the band and then back at me.

"Aren't these the same guys that were at the bar the other
night?" he asked.

"Yeah," I said loudly over the singing. "Captain Caraway and
the Seeded Ryes. They play everywhere in the area."

"Captain Caraway and the Seeded Ryes? That's really the name
of the band?"

I guess he has a fondness for rye bread," I answered Damian.
"I'm sure if I ever get around to bread making I'll see him all
the time in the bakery."

"You want to grow the business then?"

"Of course. I think if I had more space I could do much more here. I would love to do bread, but what I really want is the space and the staff to do cakes and cake decorating. I always loved doing that when I was studying to be a pastry chef. I still make some cakes on the side, usually out of my house because we just don't have the room in the shop, but someday we will."

Damian grinned at me as he leaned back in his chair.

"What?" I asked. "I know I'll get there. It's just going to take some time."

"I don't doubt it for a minute. You have the talent, the strength, and the smarts. I can see you running a bakery empire one day."

"I don't need an empire." I picked up the menu and started to look it over. "I just want a little piece to make me happy."

Our waitress, a young blonde woman wearing the nametag of Wendy who I had seen in the bakery many times, came over and took our drink order. Damian and I went back to reading the menu, which was filled with some great choices of food with a Caribbean flair. I could already smell the crab cakes I planned to order, knowing that they were fresh and made perfectly here.

After we ordered food, Damian and I kicked back, mixing conversation and drink with listening to the band. The band mixed in a little of everything, with classic rock, country, oldies, and even a little reggae Captain Caraway style filled the room. I opened up to Damian and told him more about life than I ever expected to say to someone I had known for just a few days.

We had each ordered the crab cakes, and after devouring them and the perfectly-cooked fries that came with them, I pushed my chair away from the table a bit so I could breathe. Captain Caraway had just started up with his version of "My Girl" when Damian rose from the table and stood next to me.

"Come on," he said, holding out his hand for me to take. "Let's dance."

Before I even had the chance to decline, he had whisked me off my feet and out onto the dance floor. Damian held my body close to his, putting one hand on my hip as we danced. I was no great dancer to start with, but in Damian's arms, I suddenly felt like Ginger Rogers. He moved me around the dance floor with ease, leading perfectly. He was far from the men I had danced with before that did the typical box steps while looking at their feet.

"You know how to dance, don't you?" I said to him as I looked up while trying not to trip over my own feet.

"Guilty as charged," he answered. "My mother made me take dancing lessons when I was a teenager. She said boys need to know how to dance to impress a lady. I got made fun of mercilessly for it, but when it came to school dances, all the girls wanted to dance with me."

"So, you were quite the ladies' man even back then, huh?"

I laid my head against his chest as we kept dancing, listening to the beating of Damian's heart as we moved. He had moved his hand up to the middle of my back, holding me tightly against him now. I relished being held in his arms this way and was disappointed when the song came to an end. The music stopped, and we stopped moving as people clapped, but Damian just looked down at me and stared right into my eyes.

"Are you ready to go?" he said softly.

I simply nodded up at him, and we walked back over to the table so he could pay the check and I could grab my purse. I was giddy when he took my hand to lead me through the crowded room now, and I caught a glimpse of Susan as we were headed for the door and gave her a smile. She gave me a thumbs up and then made an avid gesture to call her, letting me know she had to know more about my date.

We got in the truck, with Damian holding the door open for me as I climbed in.
"Well, it's your choice where we go from here," I said to him as I brushed the hair from my eyes.

"Okay," he said to me.

The sun was just starting to set some as we drove along and back towards Bethany Beach. Within minutes we were turning towards his house and entering the driveway through the gate. The limo was still neatly parked where it had been the last time I had seen it, and Damian pulled the truck into the garage, giving me a glimpse of the other cars he had in there.

Damian took our bags from the truck and carried them into the house. We hopped in the small elevator on the first floor and began to ride up. I started feeling very warm in the elevator, with the combination of the closeness to Damian, the drinks of the day, the smallness of the room and the feelings I was having all driving up my body temperature. We stopped on the second floor and got out, walking over towards the pool.

"Want to go for a swim?" Damian asked me as he opened the door to enter the pool area.

"Sure, that sounds like fun." We hadn't really gone swimming today, but I knew my suit was probably still damp from going to Seacrets.

"I'm just going to run upstairs and change," Damian said to me. "You can change in any of the rooms here, or out in the cabana if you like."

"Thanks."

I picked up my bag and walked passed the indoor area of the pool to the outside and entered the cabana. The cabana itself was quite large, maybe even bigger than my bedroom at home, and it held a couch, a closet filled with towels, a full sink and toilet, and even some lockers for storage.

I rifled through my bag and pulled out my damp bathing suit, taking a close look at it. I then remembered the bikini Jodie had packed in my bag also and decided to put it on. It might be more revealing than I had wanted it to be, but it was dry.

I stripped out of my dress and underwear and pulled the bikini bottoms on, making sure they fit nicely on my hips. I put the halter top on, tying it behind my neck, and then put my hair up into a ponytail, so it was out of the way. I looked at myself in the mirror on the back of the door to the cabana and adjusted the top, so it fit more comfortably and gave me a bit ampler cleavage than what I usually show.

I felt nervous for the first time in a long time and in a way I didn't typically feel. I never cared much about the way people saw me or what they thought about my looks. They accepted me for who I am, and that was that. I wasn't going out of my way to impress anyone. But now I found myself checking and double checking how I looked, something I never did, and I almost felt hypocritical about it.

I grabbed two towels from the cabana and walked out to the pool area. Even though it was still warm outside, I immediately felt a chill hit my exposed skin. I moved quickly to the indoor area of the pool and saw Damian wasn't back yet. I sat on the edge of the pool, dangling my feet in the warm water, trying to play out in my head just what was going to happen the rest of the evening.

I heard the door open and saw Damian walking through. He was dressed in black swim trunks, showing off his body once again. My gaze followed him as he placed some items on the chairs where I had put the towels. He came over to me and sat next to me, handing me a glass bottle of water.

"I thought you might want something that wasn't alcohol today," he said with a smile.

"Good idea," I told him. "Glass bottles by the pool? You're living dangerously."

"I know, but they are better than having those horrible plastic bottles of water around. At least these get recycled properly. My company is working on alternatives to plastic bottles for water, so hopefully, we can come up with something that is affordable and won't pollute the earth. My scientists think…"

I put my hand up to Damian's lips to quiet him.

"Let's swim, Damian," I said to him with a smile.

I stood up and walked over to the steps leading down into the pool. I watched as Damian eyed me as I moved along, getting his first view of me in the bikini. It felt incredible to know he was watching every step I took from the time I rose to when I gingerly went down the steps and into the cool water.

I moved over in front of where he was still sitting on the edge, ducking under the water to get my hair wet before popping back up.

"Are you getting in?" I asked him.

"I'll be there in a minute."

"This was your idea, remember?" I said to him.

I playfully splashed at him a couple of times to get him wet and then I saw him jump up. I swam quickly over towards where the inside portion of the pool led to the outside, hoping to beat him to the area, but he had jumped in and caught up to me right away. I let out a slight yell as I felt Damian grab at my foot as I tried to swim from him, but he grabbed me and then pulled me towards him.

We were standing face to face, in that in-between area of the two sections of the pool. My heart was racing, and I was breathing a little harder as Damian stared at me with intensity in his eyes.

"That bikini…" he said quietly. "You look amazing."

I placed my hands on his smooth chest, walking him back closer to the wall of the pool. When I felt his back bump the wall, Damian moved closer to me, bending down and kissing me lightly at first. Instinct took over, and I pushed against him, pressing my body to him closer than it had ever been.

Damian's hands moved down from my shoulders, across my ribs and rested on my hips. We kept kissing, with greater and greater intensity. It wasn't long before his hands were working back up my body and untying my bikini top. He let the laces fall, and the small triangles of fabric covering my breasts quickly fell with them. My nipples perked up right away as I felt the water hit them directly, and once Damian had placed his right hand on my breast, caressing it as he kissed my lips, the rest of my body reacted just as strongly to him.

Both of his hands traced my breasts, his thumbs gliding over my nipples deftly. My moans were stifled by the kissing that seemed relentless, and my hands were looking for places to go as they roamed his muscular back, chest, and abs. Every inch I touched was toned and strong, and when my hands worked inside his trunks, untying the drawstring so I could reach inside, I didn't find anything different. I grasped his erection in my fist, moving my fist up slowly, and Damian growled hungrily, kissing my neck and shoulder while toying with my nipples. The more I stroked, the deeper his breathing was getting, and then I felt his hands slide down, tugging at my bikini bottoms to move them down my legs.

Damian had managed to get them down past my thighs before I could wiggle out of them myself, and his hand pressed tightly up against my sex as I kept stroking him. When that first finger slipped inside me, I groaned loudly and felt my knees get weak. I was more than ready for him before, and my body ached to have him.

Damian pulled his hand away from me and tugged down his swim trunks. I saw them bob up in the water next to us out of the corner of my eye before he placed his hands on my hips and pulled my wet, naked body to his. He spun me around, putting my back up against the wall of the pool, and his erection slid easily inside me. I wrapped my legs around his waist, holding onto his shoulders as he penetrated me time and again. The movements were slow and in rhythm at first, and soon I was moving up and down on him, my nipples hovering just above the water, electricity shooting through them and down with each movement he took inside me.

It had been so long since I experienced anything like this that I didn't know how long I could make it last. My body started to feel hotter and hotter even though we were in the cool water, and my legs gripped Damian tightly. Each thrust Damian made brought me closer and closer to the edge, and I heard myself panting. Damian sensed how close I was and looked me in the eyes as he moved. My arms stretched out on the pool edge as he withdrew from me slowly and then just slowly pushed back in. My hands slid along the wet marble edge, and my fingernails scraped along as I gasped. When I felt I couldn't hold out any longer as he thrust deeply into me, I reached over, grabbed Damian around the neck and kissed him hard, moaning into his mouth as the orgasm washed over me.

My pussy throbbed around him, my body held him tightly, and it was then I felt Damian tense up and push into me as he came. His fingers gripped my back, and he kissed me over and over before he rested his head on my shoulder as I lay against the wall of the pool. I eased my legs from around his waist as the muscles were on fire, and I gave him gentle kisses on the neck as my fingers pawed through his wet hair.

Damian started to pull away from me slowly, but my shaking hands reached out to hold him there.

"Don't leave just yet," I whispered to him. "My legs are like jelly. I might just sink to the bottom and stay there."

Damian took me in his arms and walked me over to the steps so I could sit.

"We didn't really do much swimming," I said to him with a smile, still working on catching my breath.

"I guess we didn't. I suppose that's my fault. Being with you all day, seeing how beautiful you are, I just couldn't help myself. I had hoped the day might end this way."

"Well, it was your idea to go swimming. That last move was my decision. Those were the rules of the day." I reached over and grabbed the pieces of my bikini as they floated near and bundled them up in my hands.

"So, I guess that means I get to decide what happens next," Damian said with an impish grin.
"And what did you have in mind?"

Damian climbed out of the pool and walked his naked body over to where the towels were. I watched him move, marveling at his physique once again, and I started to stir inside again.

Damian offered his hand to me as he helped me stand up on my still wobbly legs. He wrapped a towel around my shoulders, slowly drying me off, and then handed me a fluffy white robe he had brought down with him. I slid the large robe on and let it envelop me, happy for the warmth it was bringing.

"Are your things in the cabana?" Damian asked me. I simply nodded and watched as he walked out to the cabana, still naked, to get my bag. On his way back, I saw him look up and move a little faster than he had been before as if someone had seen him.

"James is back," he said with a laugh. "We might want to take the elevator up."

Damian put a robe on, took my bag and we both hustled out of the pool area to the elevator. The elevator door closed and it moved slowly up to the top floor. Damian stood behind me, kissing my neck the whole ride up, his hands slipping around my waist and inside my robe to feel my bare flesh.

When the elevator doors opened, Damian peeked out first to make sure no one was upstairs. Nodding that it was clear, I dashed out of the elevator and over towards his room. Damian quickly followed, his robe swinging open as he got in the room and closed the door.

I sat back on the king-size bed, feeling the comfortable mattress beneath me. Damian tossed my bag on a chair in the room and sat next to me on the bed before pulling me back, so I was lying next to him. He started kissing me again, untying the front of my robe so he could pull the sides open and lightly run his fingers over my body.

"Spend the night with me," Damian said softly as he started kissing my shoulder.

"Damian, I have to open the bakery tomorrow, I can't..." My voice trailed off as his kissing had worked its way down to my breasts and he placed light kisses on each one.

"You can spend the night and still get to the bakery in time to open," he said to me as he kept kissing my breasts. "You have plenty of clothes, and I'll make sure to set the alarm, so you get up. Please, I really want you to stay. I want to wake up with you."

"I don't know," I said, almost breathlessly as Damian's kissing was now working its way lower, across my stomach to my waist.

"It's my choice to decide what's next, remember?" Damian was looking at me now from between my legs, kissing the inside of my left thigh. My body and will melted again.

"Okay, I'll stay," I said to him. "But that means I decide what happens now."

"Oh? So, what happens next?"

I shot Damian a smile as I saw his face between my legs. I reached down, taking the back of his head, and guided his face towards me. When I felt his lips and tongue dart inside me, I knew I had made the right decision for the next step.

14

Damian

When I heard the rapid beeping of a cell phone, I was jolted out of my restful sleep. Spending the night with my arms draped around Kelly, holding her close, had given me a sense of peace and happiness I haven't felt for a long time in my personal life. We had spent the night exploring each other, and it was deep into the night before we had finally exhausted ourselves and curled up together in the sheets of my bed.

My eyes were open, barely, when I saw Kelly crawl out from my arms and walk to the bathroom. I could see her shapely body move across the room as just the barest hint of light was making its way through the blinds on the windows. I heard the water in the shower start to thrum and rolled onto my back as I considered getting up and joining Kelly in the shower. My body yearned to be near her again.

The shower didn't last long, and Kelly appeared in the doorway of the bathroom, a blue towel wrapped tightly around her. She was surprised when she saw me sitting up in the bed, anticipating her coming back.

"I hope I didn't wake you," she said as the steam slowly escaped from the bathroom into the bathroom.

Kelly walked over to her bag and sorted through the items she had so she could get some clean clothes to put on.

"It's fine," I said to her, smiling as I watched her pull her panties up her legs.

Kelly looked over her shoulder at me and saw me staring at her. She gave me a sly smile, turning around completely and then leaning over to me on the bed to kiss me. Kelly pressed her breasts against my chest, and my arms went around her, trying to pull her back into bed with me.

Kelly slowly broke our kiss and gasped a little. "Damian, I have to get dressed. I need to go to the bakery."

"Can't you just take one day?" I pleaded, as my fingertips gently grazed her bare breasts as she moved away from me.

"It's my business," Kelly said as she put her bra on. "People are counting on me to be there and work. I'm sure it's the same with your company. You don't just take days off when you have responsibilities."

"I'm here right now because I needed a break from business. Sometimes you just have to get away to clear your head, do other things, see what you have been missing. You don't want the world to completely pass you by. If I hadn't taken some time to myself, I never would have met you."

Kelly sat on the bed next to me, now dressed in a pair of jeans and a t-shirt. She tied her hair back into a ponytail and then took my hand.

"I know Damian, and these last few days have been wonderful for me. You have helped me see what I have been missing out on, but I need to find a way to balance that out with the rest of my life. The bakery is important to me, and I can't just not show up and leave everyone short like that. My family relies on me to be there. You can understand that, can't you? I would love to crawl back in bed with you, I really would. You have

no idea how strong the temptation is to do that, but I have to get back to the real world."
Kelly kissed me lightly before I pulled back from her.

"The real world?" I said to her, looking into her eyes. "What has the last two days been for you? I know for me, it's been the most real the world has been in a long time. I don't just go around trying to bed women, Kelly, no matter what newspapers and social media might like people to think about me." I turned and got out of bed, grabbing a pair of shorts off the floor and pulling them on.

Kelly walked over to me, putting her arms around my waist from behind me and pulling me to her as I opened the blinds to catch a glimpse of the faint hints of sunrise starting to show.

"Damian, I didn't mean it the way it came out. Of course, this has been real for me. Trust me, I don't just do things like this either, but it has all seemed like a dream to me. It's not every day a girl gets swept up like this outside of what you might see in the movies or read in a book. Things like this don't happen in our little beach town, but I'm glad it's happening to me."

I turned around and took Kelly in my arms, kissing her deeply. I understood what she said and knew there was nothing I could do to convince her to stay.

"Do you want me to walk you to the bakery?" I asked her.

Kelly walked over and gathered her purse and put her bag over her shoulder.

"That's alright," she said to me. "I'm used to doing it. There's nobody out there right now besides early morning joggers and fishermen."

"I can at least walk you out," I told her as I opened the bedroom door.

We both slowly walked to the stairs, and I took the bag from her so I could carry it down. We went down the stairs as quietly as we could, and I stepped outside with Kelly and felt the cool air hit my bare chest. A rainstorm had come through last night and cooled things down considerably, and I felt the cold dampness on the soles of my feet as I padded onto the driveway with Kelly. I pressed the button to open the gate so she could get out.

"Thank you for an amazing time," Kelly said to me, kissing me once more.

"I should say the same to you," I replied. "I'll come by the bakery later today, around the end of the workday."

"That would be nice." Kelly grinned at me and then started to walk up the driveway towards the gate.

I watched her the entire way, and she did glance back to see me watching her and let out a small laugh. She turned right outside the gate to make her way to the boardwalk, and I went back inside. I already started thinking about her and what we might want to do after work.

I went back to my room, shut the door and got back into bed. I rolled onto my side and suddenly felt very tired. I had gotten only about two hours or so of sleep, and my body reacted to it. I closed my eyes and drifted off, catching a whiff of the scent Kelly had left on the pillow, a wonderful reminder for me.

I woke several hours later as the sun was peering strongly through the open blinds now. I looked at my watch on my nightstand to see it was after ten. I audibly groaned and rolled to the other side of the bed, still getting the faint smell of Kelly that brought a smile to my face.

After about five minutes of just lazing in bed, I got out and into a hot shower. My muscles did ache a little from all the activity of the previous day, but it was certainly a good ache. When I got out of the shower and walked over to the mirror so I could shave, I noticed that Kelly must have made a note in the steam on the mirror when she showered earlier. There was a small heart shape in the top left corner and a smiling face. I left the images there, wiping the rest of the fog from the mirror so I could shave.

I dressed and went out to the kitchen and saw that thankfully there was already a pot of coffee made. I poured a mug, taking in the aroma, and looked to see James and Shannon both sitting outside on the deck. I walked out to join them, interrupting their laughing. Both turned to me immediately when they saw me.

"There's the late riser," Shannon said, peering at me over her sunglasses.

"Good morning," I said, pulling over one of the wooden deck chairs to sit next to them.

"I guess you had a good day yesterday," Shannon spoke. She sipped her own coffee, letting out another little laugh.

"We had a great time," I announced, not saying anything more.

"Ah, a man a few words. You're always the gentleman, Damian. Women don't like a man who brags about his… for lack of a better word, dalliances."

"What's that supposed to me?" I said defensively.

"Well, I know I heard two sets of footsteps coming down the stairs and opening the front door early this morning, so I assume you had a guest here. Don't get upset, Damian, I was just teasing you. Boy, you're all sensitive now that you have a girlfriend. Maybe the brooding billionaire was better."

I could see Shannon smiling at James.

"Very funny," I said to her. "So, what did you two do all day yesterday? Did you have a good time?"

"You name it, we did it yesterday," James said. "Shannon had me driving all over the area to see and do whatever we came across. We went to the nature preserves, the lighthouse, spent time at the beach, went on a boat ride, a little of everything."

"Yes, Sarge was great," Shannon remarked. "He was willing to go along with whatever I saw as we drove. I have lots of great pictures. How about you and Kelly?"

"We had a great time. We went for a balloon ride, lounged in the water at a local place, had dinner, did some dancing, and then came back here for a swim and to hang out. It might be the best date I ever had."

"So, are you seeing her again today?" James asked me, as he finished off his coffee.

"She's working today, but I told her I would stop by when the bakery closes so we could get together. I hope you two are okay with that. I know this is a vacation for all of us, and I haven't really spent much time with you guys."

"It's not a problem, Boss," James said as he got up. "You're here to relax and have a good time, with or without us. Need a refill?"

"Thanks," I said, handing James my mug.
"How about you?" James said to Shannon.

"You bet, Sarge," she told him with a smile.

James went inside to get more coffee, and Shannon turned to me, taking her sunglasses off.

"You're really taken with Kelly, aren't you? I can see it on your face every time you talk about her. I've never seen you light up like this, Damian."

"She's unlike any other woman I have met, Shannon. When I'm with her… I just feel fantastic. It doesn't matter what we are doing, or where we go, and when I'm not with her, all I can think about is when I am going to see her again."

"I don't mean to put a damper on your romance, Damian," Shannon said to me as she picked up her phone. "Paul is getting pretty insistent about speaking with you. He keeps calling me and texting me and did it all day yesterday. He said he keeps trying to get in touch with you, but you never answer him."

"Because I've been ignoring him and having a good time instead; like you should."

"I get that we're on vacation, Damian, but it must be something important for him to keep at it like this. Maybe you should just give him a call."

"Knowing Paul, it's a leaky faucet in the men's room that needs fixing, and he wants my approval first. I'm sure it can wait. There's nothing that could come along that is so desperate he needs my attention. If it were bad, one of the other execs would be calling you or me. I'll get back to him eventually. For now, I am having too good of a time to worry about work stuff."

James reappeared, passing out coffee mugs to us. The three of us sat silently for a few minutes, just looking out over the ocean.

"Any thoughts about what to do this afternoon?" James asked.

"Let's fill one of the coolers with beer, go down by the pool, fire up the grill for lunch, and just hang out," I said.

"Now that's a plan I can get behind!" Shannon said, springing up out of her chair. "I'm going to put my suit on. I'll meet you two down by the pool. Don't forget the cooler."

"I guess I'll go fill the cooler," James said.

I kept staring out over the water, drinking my coffee, thinking about the balloon ride from yesterday.

"You okay, Boss?" James picked up his coffee mug and stood next to me.

"I'm fine," I told him, snapping myself out of my daydream. "I'll be down at the pool after I get my bathing suit on.

"I've got to tell you," James started, "this is the happiest I have seen you, well since I started working for you."

James walked into the house, and I sat on the deck, watching and orange and yellow kite flutter in the breeze just off to my right down the beach.

It is the best I've been, no doubt about it, I thought to myself.

15

Kelly

The walk to the bakery never felt better for me. I moved quickly towards the shop, bouncing along with energy I rarely had early in the morning. The last two days with Damian had been truly special and had given me much to look forward to. My mind was suddenly filled with ideas for the shop and for me, both professionally and personally. I was inspired like never before, and I was grinning ear to ear as I walked along. I even said a friendly "hello" to a few of the early morning joggers and fishermen I passed on my way to the bakery. I got some odd looks, but I didn't care a bit.

I got closer to the bakery and noticed the T-Shirt Cabana, the t-shirt and souvenir store next to us, wasn't just closed as it normally would be this time of the morning. The storm gate had been pulled down over the front of the store, something they never did unless there was impending bad weather coming.

That's odd, I thought to myself as I gazed at the gate and the closed sign hanging on it. Harry Chapman, the owner of the store, was one of the nicest guys on the boardwalk and always had a smile, kind word, or helping hand for business people and the community. He and his family had the shop for many years and were the best neighbors. I hoped everything was okay with him and his family as I turned the corner to get to the rear of the bakery.

The back door was already unlocked when I arrived, meaning someone was already here and starting to open. I felt guilty about being a bit later and knew I was going to get all kinds of questions about it as soon as I walked into the kitchen.

Jodie was there getting the ovens going, and I could smell the first batch of cinnamon buns underway already, the distinct smell filling the air in the kitchen. Jodie had the music turned up loud enough where she didn't even hear me enter, so I just grabbed an apron and got ready to get started. I heard an audible gasp when Jodie turned and saw me standing there.

"Shit, Kelly, you could have at least made some noise when you came in," Jodie said, juggling the canisters she had in her hands and placing them on the table.

I went over and turned the music down a bit so we could hear each other without yelling.

"Sorry, I just slipped in under the music I guess."

I looked around and saw a bunch of pastries already prepared and ready to go for the day.

"What time did you get here this morning? I didn't think I was this late," I asked her as I looked at the racks filled with cookies and donuts.

"Oh, I couldn't sleep last night, so I came in a few hours ago and got things started. I just had some energy I guess." Jodie wiped her hands on her apron and looked over at me with a grin.

"So, I guess yesterday went pretty well, huh?"

"What makes you say that?" I answered coyly.

"Well, you never came by to claim your dog last night, and you're still carrying the bag of clothes we packed yesterday, so you never made it home either. It's pretty easy to figure out where you ended up."

"Jodie, it was an amazing day," I said to her, moving closer to her so we could talk.

I told her all about our adventures in the balloon, the good time we had at Seacrets, and then how we spent the rest of the night together.

"He's nothing like I thought he would be, Jodie," I explained to her. "You think about the typical rich guys that come down here, and Damian is just the opposite. He's not hung up on money, or showing off, or bragging. He's a gentleman, he's caring, but he's strong when he wants to be or needs to be."

"I guess so by the way you said that," Jodie added with a laugh.

"Oh, he definitely knows how to take charge."

"Take charge of what?" I heard from behind us and spun around to see Mom and Alex coming through the door.

"These donuts," I offered, trying to cover up as quickly as I could. I grabbed the tray of donuts that needed to be filled with jelly and moved them over to one of the free tables.

"Jodie has left these sitting here without filling them, so I'm taking charge of them." I grabbed a pastry bag and quickly filled it with some of our raspberry jam and start pressing it gently into the donuts.

"Mmmm, Hmmm," Mom said with her knowing look as she hung up her coat. She walked out to the storefront to start things out there while Alex stayed and put on her apron.

"You were talking about your date yesterday, weren't you?" she said quietly. "What happened?"

"Alex, this isn't really the time to get into all of that. All I will say is that we had a lovely time and I hope to get to see him again."

"Really?" Alex replied with a pout. "That's all you're going to tell me, but you have no problem telling Jodie the details? That's pretty shitty, Kelly."

"Alexandra, language please!" Mom shouted from the store. Alex rolled her eyes and trudged out to the store to help Mom.

"She's going to be mad at you, you know," Jodie stated.

"I know, but what does she expect me to do? Go into details with Mom standing right there?"

"I think you need to give her a little more credit, Kel." Jodie walked over from her station and stood next to me. "I think she gets jealous a lot because we're so close. She feels a little left out of the sister stuff at times."

"Okay, I get it." I finished filling the jelly donuts and brought them out to the shop.

Mom was taking the chairs down from off the tables while Alex prepped the coffee station. I carried the tray over to the display case and began to fill the area with donuts.

"Alex, can you go grab the other tray for me?" I asked her. She looked over at me and stomped off into the kitchen to get the other tray.

It was difficult for me with Alex sometimes because of the age difference between us. Jodie was only a couple of years' difference with me, but Alex was several, and it seemed like there was a big gap between us at times in a lot of ways. I never meant for her to be excluded, and it was tough for me to think of her as a young woman now and not just the little kid that was always getting into my stuff.

Alex came out with a tray filled with frosted chocolate donuts, glazed donuts, and plain donuts and placed it on the counter next to me. She started to move back towards the coffee when I asked her to help me fill the case. I looked over at Mom, who saw what I was doing, and shifted my eyes toward the kitchen. Mom took the hint and went in to help Jodie.

"Alex, I'm sorry, I didn't mean to…"

"Be insensitive?" she interrupted. "I get it, Kelly. I've been dealing with it my whole life."

"Hey, that's not fair," I said to her. I stepped back from the display case and leaned on the back counter, staring at Alex. "You have to understand that Jodie and I are close in age. We relied on just each other for years before you were born. It's just different is all. I know I act too much like the oldest sister at times, and I don't treat you like the young adult you are now, and I'm sorry about that. I promise to be better about it, okay?"

I put my arm around Alex after she filled the case and pulled her to me, making sure to wipe some of the powdered sugar that was on my gloved hands right on her chin.

"Does that mean you'll tell me about your date?" she asked me.

"I will, I promise, but not right now, not with Mom here. It feels… weird."

Mom came walking out of the kitchen with a tray of warm pastries.

"You know, you three go around hiding all this talk about boys, men, dates, sex, and whatever from me like I don't know anything about it," she said calmly as she placed pastries in the case. "Where do you think you three came from? The stork didn't deliver you, you know."

"Ugh, Mom," Alex answered, crinkling her face in disgust. "I don't want to hear about you and Dad."

"Go get the rest of the trays," Mom said to Alex, shooing her into the kitchen and giving her a light swat with a towel as Alex sped by.

Mom walked over to me as I was looking over the cases to see what else we might need for the day.

"Did you have a nice time, honey?" she asked me as she wiped down the counter.

"I did Mom, it was great," I said to her.

"I'm glad to hear it. It's been so long since you started seeing someone. Do you want to come over for dinner tonight? I'm making your favorite – chicken parmesan."

"You know I can't resist your chicken parm. Of course, I'll be there."

Once the bakery was opened, it was the usual madness of a Tuesday morning. Locals and visitors rushed in and out to get coffee, donuts, pastries, and snacks, and we were kept moving for hours. The morning quickly vanished and spread into the early afternoon before things started to slow down. I seemed to have boundless energy and kept moving, getting things prepped, baked, and out to the shop. I even took a turn working the register and helping customers when it looked like Mom could use a break.

After the early afternoon rush died down and closing time was nearing, I saw Damian walk in. He was wearing a dark green polo shirt that clung nicely to his body, and a pair of khaki shorts that looked just as nice on him. I smiled as soon as I saw him and watched him walk towards the counter.

"Hi there," he said to me with a big grin.

The room suddenly felt ten degrees warmer to me just from the look he gave me.

"Hey," I said trying to be casual, but I knew I had a huge smile on my face.

"I just thought I would drop by and see if you had any jelly donuts left." Damian scanned over to the display case with the donuts, and there wasn't much left in there.

"I don't think we have any left," I said to him. I could see he looked disappointed, but then his gaze turned back to me, and he smiled again.

"That's okay. I'm sure I don't really need them anyway," Damian said as he patted his firm stomach.

"I might have a few left in the back," I said, pointing to the kitchen doors and I started to move to go look. Damian reached out and grabbed my hand, holding it, to keep me in place.

"Don't bother," he said to me. "I didn't really come in looking for donuts. I just wanted to see you and see if you were free tonight."
The heat turned up even more as he held my hand. Damian's index finger lightly stroked mine, and it made my heart race.

"I would love to," I replied. I then snapped out of my haze. "Oh, wait, I'm supposed to go to my Mom's for dinner tonight. You know, a sisters-daughters-Mom kind of bonding thing."

Damian looked disappointed, but Mom then popped up right behind me as he held my hand.

"Damian, you are more than welcome to join us for dinner if you like. It's nothing fancy; just a home-cooked meal," Mom chimed in.

I looked back at Damian, expecting him to politely say no. Why would he eat a chicken parm dinner in Mom's cramped house when he could eat anything he wants at his place?

"I would love a home-cooked meal," he answered. Part of me was thrilled that he accepted, and another part of me nervous about him getting grilled by my sisters.

"Great!" Mom exclaimed. "We close up here in a bit. Come on by around five. I'm sure Kelly can show you the way."

I came out from behind the counter and walked with Damian as he moved toward the front door.

"You don't have to come if you don't want to," I said to Damian, trying to give him an out.

"I really want to come," he said seriously. "I want to get to know your family. It will be fun."

"You think so, huh?" I said sarcastically. "Be prepared for what my sisters have to bring."
Damian let out a chuckle. "You'd be surprised what kind of questions I have been asked over the years, Kelly. I don't think they can throw anything at me that I haven't heard before."

"Don't let them hear you say that," I warned. "They'll take that as a challenge."

"Stop worrying about it," Damian told me. "What's the address?"

"18 Allan Drive," I told him. "I won't be offended if you don't show."

"I'll be there." Damian leaned in and kissed me, placing his hands on my waist.

I felt myself drawing closer to him as the kiss lingered. It was only the "Oooh" from my sisters that caused me to break it and shoot them a stern look while they stood laughing behind the counter. Damian just smiled down at me and ignored them.

"I'll see you at five," he told me before he walked out the door.

I closed the door behind him, locking it and flipping over the sign, so it showed "Closed." As soon as I looked towards Alex and Jodie, both started making kissing noises, wrapping their arms around each other.

"You guys are jerks. I should fire both of you," I said as I stomped towards the counter.

"If she's this worked up now, wait and see how she'll be at dinner," Alex prodded.

"If you embarrass me at all, you can be sure I will be telling Mom about your little skinny-dipping adventure with your friends two weeks ago down on the beach."

Alex looked worried for a second and then burst out laughing.

"It's okay, it will be totally worth the grounding," she said with a laugh.

"It's going to be a long night," I lamented out loud as I walked into the kitchen to clean up.

16

Damian

I went back to the house after meeting Kelly and making plans for dinner so I could change and get myself ready. I walked inside and didn't hear a sound. I called around for James and Shannon, but neither of them answered me. I even knocked on their bedroom doors but got no replies. I made my way upstairs without any sign of them before finding a note stuck to my bedroom door:

Boss,

Gone out for the night. We figured you were doing the same. See you later and have fun!

Shannon and Sarge

At least I didn't have to feel guilty about leaving them to their own devices yet again for the night. They seemed to find plenty of things to do themselves, and I was glad they were making the most of their vacation like I was.

I quickly went into the bedroom to change, putting on a simple button down shirt and a pair of shorts to go along with my sandals. I grabbed a couple of bottles of wine off the wine rack to bring with me and went down to the garage to get a car to bring with me. I saw that James and Shannon had taken the Mustang again, so I opted for the truck to get myself over to Kelly's mother's house.

Getting to the house was easy for me now that I was getting more comfortable with driving around town. I pulled into the driveway right on time and made my way from the car to the front porch in just a few strides. I knocked on the door and waited patiently for someone to answer. Kelly's sister Alex pulled open the door quickly and greeted me with a smile.

"Hiya!" she said enthusiastically, opening the screen door for me. "Come on in."

I was greeted by the familiar smell of cooking pasta and sauce and could feel the warmth coming from the kitchen. Kelly's mother Mary peeked her head around the corner and gave me a wave.

"Kelly's just getting changed," Alex said to me as we walked into the living room. She pointed towards the couch, and I took a seat. Alex positioned herself right next to me, looking like she was anxious to pepper me with questions.

"Alex, offer Damian a drink!" I heard Mary yell from the kitchen.

"Would you like something to drink?" Alex muttered.

"Sure, that would be great," I answered. "I brought some wine to go with dinner."

I handed Alex the two bottles, and she looked at them.

"Great, something else I can't have," she said with a sigh as she rose from the couch with the bottles in her hands.

She walked into the kitchen, and I heard Mary yell again from the kitchen.

"Thank you for the wine, Damian!"

"You're welcome," I yelled back, laughing.

Alex appeared again momentarily with two glasses in her hands. She handed me one tall glass and kept the other for herself.

"I hope iced tea is okay," she said, sitting next to me again.

"Perfect, thank you," I replied.

The glass sent a chill up my neck it was so cold. I took a small sip, seeing Alex watching me the whole time like I was something on television. I placed the glass on the coffee table in front of us and sat back. I saw Alex take a breath as she got ready to speak, but I noticed behind her, coming down the hall, were Kelly and Jodie.

I stood up from the couch as they entered the room. Kelly looked stunning in an olive-colored tank dress. I could not take my eyes off her as she walked over and stood in front of me.

"Wow," I said softly to her.

Kelly brushed a stray hair from her face and smiled at me.

"I told you that dress would get his attention," Alex said gleefully. Jodie promptly grabbed Alex and ushered her into the kitchen.

"Sorry about that," Kelly said. "I have to admit though, I did borrow this dress from her. I don't really have much in my closet other than jeans and t-shirts."

"I think you look great just in your jeans and t-shirt, you know," I told her.

I pulled Kelly closer to me and gave her a long, slow kiss. The kiss was finally broken when we heard a brief giggle come from the doorway to the kitchen.

"Dinner's ready," Alex said with a big grin.

Kelly took my hand and led me into the kitchen. The table was filled with food, more than the five of us could eat in one sitting for sure.

Alex patted the seat next to her. "Sit next to me Damian," she asked.

"I don't think so," Kelly said, pulling me over so I would sit next to her on the opposite side of the table. Jodie walked over to the table and placed a salad bowl filled with greens down before sitting next to Alex. Mary sat at the head of the table, smiling as everyone took their place.

Before we dug into the meal, Mary asked us all to join hands so she could say Grace. I held onto Kelly's hand tightly while Alex took my other hand as we bowed our heads.

Afterward, everyone passed around the dishes of chicken parmesan, pasta, and salad so they could fill their plates, and Mary cleared her throat to get everyone's attention.

"I would just like to say how nice it is to have my girls here, and to have you, Damian," Mary stated, holding up her wine glass. "It's pretty rare that any of the girls brings a gentleman around to the house. It's especially nice to see you doing it, Kelly."

I looked over at Kelly and could see her blushing. I simply turned back to Mary and clinked glasses with her.

"Well thank you for having me into your home," I told her.

We went through dinner very casually, much more so than I have been exposed to at any time. There was lots of laughter, smiles, and good-natured teasing among all the sisters. Before I knew it, everyone had eaten, a bottle of wine was gone, and the table was ready to be cleared.

I could see Mary giving a look to Alex, letting her know she should get up and start collecting plates. I stood up from the table to gather some things.

"Let me help," I offered.

"Sit down, Damian," Mary ordered. "The girls can take care of clearing the table and the dishes. You're a guest here. You and I can go sit in the living room and relax while they tend to the dishes and fix us some coffee, right girls?"

"I don't live here anymore," Kelly said, looking nervous about me being alone with her mother. "I'm a guest. Why do I have to clean up?"

"Because your mother asked you to," Mary said with a smile. She got up from the table, took my arm, and led me into the living room.

I sat down on the couch while Mary sat in the rocking chair posted across from me. The chair creaked lightly with each light movement she made, and for what seemed like a long time that was the only noise that passed between us.

"Are you enjoying our little town here?" Mary asked me.

"Yes, very much, at least what I have seen of it so far. It has everything I had hoped it would, and more."

"Wonderful," she said to me. "I've lived here my whole life, and I've seen it grow from a much smaller place to what it is today. Somehow, we've managed to keep it a tight community even with all that goes on during the summer."

We sat quietly again, Mary gently rocking, before Jodie appeared in the living room, carrying a tray with a coffee pot, mugs, and more. She placed it on the coffee table in front of me and smiled.

"Thank you, Jodie," Mary stated, looking at her daughter with a pleased look.

Jodie looked back at her with a serious face.

"My pleasure, Mum," she said in a broken British accent while she curtseyed.

"Go finish the dishes," Mary said to her, waving her off with a smile.

I poured a mug of coffee for Mary and handed it to her before pouring one for myself. We both took light sips, and Mary continued to rock, holding her mug.

"Damian, I know it's only been a few days, but I can tell Kelly thinks a lot of you. You do realize that, don't you?"

"I hope that's the case, Mary," I said to her. "I think a lot of her too."

"Good, I'm glad to hear that. Kelly is not one to open her heart up too easily. She never has been. The few times she has, she's been burned in the past. A man a lot like you actually – handsome, wealthy, from New York. She met him while she was in school up there. He gave her a job in one of the restaurants he owned, and she stayed there until she found out he was fooling around with the hostess. Kelly left and came back home and worked here. He had the nerve to come down and charmed her again and then broke her heart again, leaving her down here for some socialite. She's been gun shy since then Damian, and I don't blame her. I don't want to see the same thing happen to her again. Do we understand each other?"

Mary sat back in her rocker and stared at me. It was her way of letting me know she was taking care of her daughters, protecting them. This soft, genial woman had her Momma Bear side and wasn't afraid to show it to anyone, no matter who they were.

"Mary, I understand you completely," I told her. "I don't know who this other person was, but I can tell you I am not like that. I care for Kelly a great deal and would never do anything to hurt her. I promise you that."

"Okay," she said, breaking her glare and smiling again. "I'm glad I won't have to get out my shotgun. I haven't fired that thing in years."

We both laughed, mine a bit more nervously than Mary's. Kelly came walking into the room carrying a tray of cookies and a small cake on it.

"Everything okay in here?" she asked before sitting down next to me on the couch.

"Wonderful, dear," Mary said. "Damian and I were just getting to know each other a bit."

I could see Kelly biting her lip, wondering if that was a good thing or not. Alex and Jodie joined us as well, and I dutifully poured coffee for everyone while we enjoyed dessert. I had just put a chocolate chip cookie in my mouth when Alex, who was seated on the floor next to her mother, blurted out: "Damian, how much money do you have in your wallet?"

I coughed on some cookie crumbs while Kelly shot her sister a mean look.

"Alex!" Kelly yelled.

After clearing my throat, I looked at Alex.

"It's okay Kelly. You'd be surprised how many people ask me that. Honestly, I'm not even sure."

I took my wallet out of my front pocket and opened it up. I started counting silently to myself.

"432 dollars," I told her, folding the wallet back up.

"Man, I thought it would be more," she said with disappointment.

"I'm amazed I have that much in there," I told her. "I don't usually carry much cash."

"Okay, next question," Alex said. "What was it like to date this model?" She held up her cell phone, and I saw a picture of me and Jessica Mulder, a model I had dated once or twice, together on the beach. Kelly leaned over and looked at the picture and then looked at me.

"Yeah, what was it like to date her?" Kelly said as she squinted her eyes at me.

I passed the phone back to Alex.

"She was a nice person, but we only went out a couple of times. We met while we were both in Bermuda. She wasn't really for me."

I sat back on the couch, still getting a look from Kelly.

"Did you take her on your yacht?" Alex asked. "You have a yacht, don't you? I'll bet it's huge. Can you land a helicopter on it? Do you have a helicopter?"

"Alright, that's enough questions for tonight," Kelly said, standing up and taking my hand, so I was up too. "I need to get home and get to bed. We do have work tomorrow you know."

"Oh man, I have a lot more questions," Alex said. "Damian, can I have your email so I can send questions to you?

"Forget it, Alex," Kelly yelled, dragging me towards the front door.

"Thank you for a lovely dinner, Mary," I said as Kelly kept pulling me. I held onto the door frame so I could say goodbye before I was outside.

Kelly pulled me down the front steps and over towards my truck. She leaned against the passenger door and brought me straight to her. Before I could say anything, she gave me a kiss.

When we finally broke the kiss, we were both breathless.

"I think I need a ride home," she said to me, reaching for the passenger door. She made sure to rub her body against mine as she slid past me and into the truck.

I got in the driver's side and drove the short distance to Kelly's home. She hopped out of the truck before I could even get the engine shut off, and I watched her as she strode from the driveway to her front door, looking back over her shoulder to make sure I watched her the whole way. By the time I got to the front door, she had already gone inside, and I saw the shoes she had kicked off marked her pathway from the hall to her bedroom.

"Sorry for the mess," she said as she kicked a small pile of clothes to the corner before she sat down on her bed. She slowly undid the few buttons on her dress, showing off her cleavage to me as she reclined on the bed.

"I didn't even notice it," I said to her, getting on the bed next to her. I moved to kiss her, and she playfully gave me a short kiss on the lips before pulling away. She did this several times, making each kiss last a bit longer than the next before she stopped, teasing me to no end. Kelly finally let me kiss her longer and deeper as she lay back completely on the bed.

My right hand went and undid the remaining buttons at the top of her dress, exposing the white lace bra she was wearing underneath. My fingers lingered on the lace trim cupping her breasts while we kissed before I reached out to cup her breast myself, grazing my thumbs gently back and forth over her nipples. She gasped lightly in my mouth as we kissed more and she pushed her body closer to mine.

Kelly's left hand had snaked down and worked open my belt and shorts, and then swiftly went inside, gripping me through my briefs. She stroked me firmly and took my breath away as her fingers worked over me. She then surprised me and rolled quickly so that she was on top of me, as she kept her hand on me the whole time. She took both hands and moved them up my body, unbuttoning my shirt so that she could move her hands over my abs and chest.

Kelly bent down and started to kiss me, kissing me on the lips before she planted slow kisses across my chest. Her hands kept touching me as her mouth moved down my body.

"Your muscles are so… hard," she said with a sly smile, moving her body, so her knees were on either side of my waist. I wanted her badly and moved my hands over her sides and up to her breasts.

Kelly quickly moved away from my hands.

"Uh uh," she said to me. "This is my game tonight."

With that she moved off me and stood up, staring at me. My eyes were locked on hers as I watched every move she made. Her hands started at her breasts, gliding over the cups of her bra and down to her hips. I watched as she slipped her hands underneath her dress, pulling her panties down her legs. She stepped out of the panties and climbed back onto the bed, kneeling between my legs.

"There's nothing quite like strong, hard muscles," Kelly whispered.

Her hands started at my knees, and I could feel the palms of her hands go over my thighs and come to rest at my waist before they tugged on my briefs, and pulled them down my legs until they were off me.

Kelly kept her eyes on me again as she moved against me. I could feel the hem of her dress brush against my erection as she moved. She rested her warm wetness against me, taking my breath away for a moment. A playful smile crossed her face as she slowly started to move, allowing her to slide over me without taking me inside her.

I moved my hands down to her waist, trying to hold her in place so I could go inside her, feel her, but her game wasn't over just yet.

"Play nice, Mr. Woods," Kelly purred at me as she pulled her body away from me. I put my hands back down to my sides and let her take over once again.

Satisfied that I was willing to go along with her, Kelly moved closer to me once again, letting me just barely feel her. The blood pounded loudly in my head with each movement she made, making me ache for her even more.

"Kelly, you're making me crazy," I groaned.

"I think that's a good thing," she replied, gliding against me once more.

I felt her hips start to slowly gyrate against me as she rocked back and forth. A quick glance up at Kelly revealed that her eyes were closed now as she moved. She had found a sweet, sensitive spot and made the most of it while I barely hung on. Finally, she allowed me in and drew me slowly inside her. Kelly kept up her slow rocking as she tightened and relaxed on me.

Each motion elicited deep groans from me that I had never let out before.

Beads of sweat formed on my brow as I couldn't take much more. My grip tightened on the fabric of Kelly's dress over her thighs, and I pulled her closer so I was deeper inside her. That was all I could take and felt my orgasm overtake me. Kelly gasped as she felt me spasm inside her and her thighs tightened around my waist, holding herself still as her own orgasm spread throughout her body.

My body was still shaking a bit when Kelly pressed herself against me and kissed me. She laid her head on my chest as we each tried to catch our breath a bit.

"Hmmm," Kelly hummed as she nuzzled herself into the nape of my neck. "That was pretty good."

"Pretty good?" I said as I chased my breath. "That was… you were… I can't even think of the words for it." I kissed Kelly on the top of her head as I wrapped my arms around her.

"I'm glad I can make you speechless."

"You did that and more."

After a few minutes, Kelly got up from the bed, stripping off what was left on of her dress to throw on a t-shirt and got back into bed with me. I put my arm around her once again.

"I hope you had a good time tonight," she said as she kissed my neck.

"You mean you couldn't tell?"

"I'm not talking about that," she said as she playfully hit my shoulder. "I mean dinner with my family. I don't usually do things like that… or like this."

"It was great, Kelly," I answered. "I loved having dinner and spending time with your family. I didn't really have the "normal" family upbringing where we all got together and had dinner and laughed and joked. Being a part of that was nice. Your mother and your sisters are great."
"Yeah, they are," she said with a sigh. Kelly closed her eyes, and I watched her as she started to drift off to sleep.

"You're pretty great, too," I said softly to her as I held her.

A small smile crept across Kelly's face as we lay silently together, holding each other.

17

Kelly

I thought it would feel funny to wake up with someone else in my bed, but instead, it was the most comforting feeling in the world for me. Damian had his arms wrapped around me when my alarm clock went off early in the morning. The temptation was great just to shut it off and crawl back to him, let myself get swept up into his arms, and spend the morning with someone like I have not done in a very long time. By the time the snooze alarm was going off for the third time, I knew I had to face the reality of getting out of bed to start my day, as much as I didn't want to.

Every time I went to pull away from his hold on me, Damian pulled me back towards him, letting me feel his naked body flush against mine. I finally turned myself around carefully, so I was facing him, my breasts pressed tightly against his chest, and I kissed him sensually enough to rouse his body and cause him to open his eyes.

"Damian, I have to get up," I said as I pulled myself away and off the bed. The cool air from the ceiling fan began to reach my naked flesh as I stood next to my dresser, causing me to shiver.

"Just stay in bed with me," he pleaded, trying to coax me back towards him.

"I have to get showered and get to the bakery." I wandered into the bathroom to turn the shower on and let the water get hot.

"Are you sure?" Damian said as he now sat up on the edge of the bed. I could see the strong definition of his muscles as he sat there, and another chill ran through me, this time making me want to get back into bed with him.

"I'm the baker, remember? If I'm not there, half of our stuff doesn't get made. Besides, mornings are when we make all our money. I'm needed there."

Damian rose from the bed and stood in the bathroom door, blocking me from entering. He had a playful grin on his face and placed his hands on my hips, pulling me towards him, so our bodies meshed once more. As we kissed, his hand moved slowly down my back until it reached my backside. He cupped my buttocks, drawing me even closer to him. My body was quivering in delight as his lips moved from my mouth to my neck.

"Damian, you have to stop…" I moaned lightly.

"Boy, you really make it hard on a guy," he said with a laugh, breaking free of me and letting me pass into the bathroom.

"I try," I said, glancing down at his obvious arousal before I closed the bathroom door.

I tried to shower quickly, but all the time I was going through the motions I thought about the man in my bedroom waiting for me. I knew I was falling quickly for him, faster than I had ever done with anyone else in my life. Normally, something like a relationship would scare me off since I was always so focused on work and my family, but there was something different with Damian, something unique and special, something I wanted to let in my life.

When I got out of the shower, I wrapped a towel around myself, expecting to go out into the bedroom and flash Damian as he lay on the bed. Unfortunately, I opened the door, and the room was empty, and my bed was made. I quickly dressed in my casual work clothes and walked out into the hallway. I immediately smelled the fresh aroma of coffee brewing and smiled.

I stood in the doorway to the kitchen and watched as Damian poured cups of coffee. Alice was sitting dutifully by his side, grateful to have a companion other than me in the morning.

"You know," I said as I walked into the kitchen, my bare feet on the cool tile floor, "I almost fell over when I saw my bed made. I rarely do that myself. Thanks."

"Old habit I have," Damian said to me as he handed me a hot mug. "My mother always made us make our beds even though we had staff in the house to do it. She said there was no reason to have someone else do what we were perfectly capable of doing ourselves."

"Smart lady," I said, sipping the hot coffee. "Unfortunately for you, you missed me standing there in just my towel."

"Now that is unfortunate." Damian put down his coffee mug and walked towards me. "Kelly, these last few days, they have been incredible. I've never wanted to be with someone like I am with you."

I put down my coffee on the counter and snuggled into his chest.

"I... I feel the same way."

I turned my face up towards Damian, and we kissed once more. Emotions were surging through me, and for a moment, I thought about forgetting about the bakery, taking his hand, and marching back into the bedroom, staying there for days. I slowly broke our kiss breathlessly and stepped back.

"I have to get moving," I said, taking a long sip of the coffee before slipping into the shoes I had by the kitchen doorway. "You're welcome to stay and finish your coffee. I'm sure Alice would love the company."

"I should probably get home myself," Damian replied. "I'll take a nap and rest myself up for later."

"And just what is going to happen later?" I asked slyly, knowing Damian was walking close behind me, watching me as I walked out the front door.

"I know what I'm hoping will happen," he said, grabbing me around the waist and lifting me up, carrying me out onto the porch. I heard myself scream a bit and start laughing, the sound echoing loudly into the early morning air.

Damian carried me down the steps and next to his truck before placing me down.

"Do you want a ride?" he asked me. I realized my scooter was still at my mother's place.

"No, it's fine. It's not like it's a long walk or anything. The morning air might do me some good anyway, help me to think clearly so I can concentrate on baking instead of..." my voice trailed off as my left hand ran down across Damian's chest once more.

"Last chance," he said to me with a smile. "We can run back inside or hop in the truck and just disappear for the day."

"Very tempting." I planted a quick kiss on his lips before I started up the driveway.

"I'll stop by the bakery later," Damian said. "Save a jelly donut for me."

"You bet," I said.

I switched on the penlight I had on my keychain so that any cars that drove by me could see me as I walked and made my way towards the boardwalk. I watched as Damian drove past me, slowing down as he went by, and I gave him a smile and a wave.

I was right – the cool air did help me clear my head some, and it wasn't long before I was thinking about what to make for the day and what needed to be done at the shop as I walked along and reached the boardwalk.

I climbed the steps about half the way to the bakery and walked on the boardwalk the rest of the way. I could see the glimmer of the sunrise just starting to peek out over the ocean, and the beauty of the orange and clear blue sky made me stop and look.

I forgot just how beautiful this place is, I thought to myself as I leaned against the boardwalk railing and looked at the sky. I could see a few birds flying against the sky, creating a picture-perfect setting.

I started on my way once again with a great bounce in my step. I came to the T-Shirt Cabana once again and saw that everything was still closed tight. The "Closed" sign had been taken down that normally hung on the front, and I wondered once again if everything was alright with Harry.

I went to the back of the bakery and tried the door and saw it was still locked, so I knew I was the first one here today. I entered and started my routine, putting my apron on, getting the ovens and machines going, taking my supplies out, and turning the radio on. I could hear myself quietly singing along, my hips swaying to the music, as I rolled out pastry dough to make turnovers.

"What has you in such a good mood this morning?" Jodie asked as she entered the kitchen.

I glanced up and smiled as I rolled out the dough to the best thickness for the turnovers before I grabbed the filling I wanted to use.

"I just love life, sis," I said to her. I spread the apple filling onto the dough and gave perfect mounding portions to each piece I planned to cut.

"You're adorable when you're getting some on a regular basis," Jodie answered as she put her apron on.

"Classy as always, Jodie."

"You wouldn't expect anything less." Jodie grabbed a few trays of cinnamon buns we had proofing in one of the refrigerators and put them out on the counter before sliding them into one of the ovens.

"I take it you had a good night last night?" Jodie asked me.

"Jodie… I can't even put it into words. Damian makes me feel like every part of my life is perfect. He doesn't judge; he likes me for me, not what I do for a living, what I look like, or where I live or how much money I have. I just want to spend time with him, and when I'm not with him, I want to be with him, you know?"

"Kelly, are you in love with him?" Jodie asked me seriously.

I stopped folding turnovers long enough to look at her as she stared at me.

"I am, Jodie. I know that sounds crazy after a few days, but I am in love with him. He's everything I want – caring, responsible, funny… and sexy as hell."

We both laughed as we went back to work, and a few minutes later Mom and Alex entered the back door, ready to start their days.

"Good morning!" I said happily while I placed the turnovers in the oven.

"Good morning to you too," Mom said with a smile as she hung up her sweater.

"Good morning, little sister," I said to Alex, patting her head as I walked past her.

"Who gave you happy pills this morning?" Alex grumbled as she walked out into the shop to start the registers.

Mom reached into her purse to pull something out and then walked over to me.

"I forgot this yesterday," she said to me, handing me a stack of mail. "I stopped by the post office yesterday to pick up the mail."

"Thanks, Mom," I said, scanning over the stack. There were plenty of advertisements and the typical invoices that didn't come in over email today. There was one large brown envelope on the bottom that I picked up and looked at, seeing it was from an address in New York.

"Did anyone notice the new surf shop that's two doors down?" Mom asked. "I saw when we walked by that the place is cleaned out and closed up. I wonder what happened."

"That's odd," I answered, running my finger under the glued flap of the envelope to open it up. "They haven't been there very long. Too bad; they were some nice guys running that place. Do you know what's up with Harry next door, Mom? The place has been closed for two days now."

"No, I haven't seen him," she yelled from the storefront.

I pulled the pages out of the envelope and looked at them. The top page was a letter on official stationery. I read over the letter again, just scanning it at first, before I stopped myself and started reading with more earnest from the top again.

Dear Ms. Barton,

This letter is to inform you that as of September 1, 2018, ownership of the building you occupy will have transferred to our company, STW Enterprises. As the new owners of this property, we would like to inform you of our intention of creating new office space for our company at your location and the adjoining locations here on the boardwalk that were purchased as part of the transaction.

We hereby give you notice that your lease has been terminated and you will have sixty (60) days to close business and vacate the premises. As an incentive for you, should you vacate within the first thirty days of this notice, you will be awarded a cash payout of $75,000.00 as thanks from us and to assist you with any relocation efforts or future endeavors.

Should you have any questions, please feel free to contact me at the phone numbers or email address listed in the header of this letter. Thank you for your attention.

Paul S. Austin
Chief Attorney, STW Enterprises

I was completely stunned. Beneath the letter were copies of my lease and pages to sign and submit should I want to vacate faster than the sixty days. I placed the papers down and just stared at them.

"What's all that?" Jodie asked as she walked over to me. "You okay, Kelly?"

"They're eviction papers," I said softly. "We're being told to get out."

"What? They can't do that. We have a lease with the management company." Jodie picked up the papers to look at the letter herself.

"Apparently, they sold the property, and the new owners want us out. Not just us, but everyone around us. We have sixty days to close."

"This can't be real," Jodie said loudly.

Mom and Alex came into the kitchen when they heard me knock an empty tray over and it clanged loudly against the floor.

"What's wrong?" Mom asked.
"They're going to make us close the bakery," Jodie said with shock, passing the letter to Mom.

Jodie, Alex, and Mom huddled near each other, reading the letter over and over as I stood in stunned silence. Everything I had worked hard for and dreamed of was dashed in just a few sentences.

"Kelly," Jodie said to me. "The company that bought the property... STW Enterprises... that's Damian's company."

I grabbed the letter from Mom's hands and looked at the letterhead. My stomach suddenly felt sour, and I wanted to throw up. I leaned over the sink for a moment as I breathed heavily. I didn't know what to feel anymore as anger, resentment, and sadness all coursed through me at once.

I stood up, calmly took off my apron, and gathered up the paperwork.

"You keep working," I said to Jodie, Mom, and Alex as I moved towards the back door.

"Where are you going?" Jodie asked.

"To see our new landlord," I growled, slamming the door behind me.

18

Damian

Leaving Kelly's place, all I could think about is how amazing it was to be with her and how lucky I was to have found her. Even though we had only known each other for days, it felt like I had made a connection with her unlike any other before. My thoughts were occupied by her image until I pulled up to the gate at my house and buzzed myself into the driveway.

I crept the truck up alongside the limo, still parked in the same spot it had been since we arrived in town. I stepped out of the truck and stretched for a minute. My muscles were aching a bit after last night and the last few days, but it was an ache I would gladly accept anytime. I made my way into the house through the garage so that I was downstairs. I tried to keep the noise down since it was still early, and James and Shannon were likely still asleep. As I shut the interior door and turned around, I saw James coming out of Shannon's room with a towel wrapped around his waist, carrying items from Shannon's room tucked under his arm. He was clearly startled and fumbled with the items he had, nearly dropping them to the floor.

"Sorry, you caught me off guard," James said, seeming unusually flustered.

"What's going on?" I asked James as I slowly started to put the situation together in my mind.

James looked straight at me and gave a bit of a grin to me. He shrugged his shoulders as he could see I knew what was going on.

"How long has that been going on?"

"Honestly boss, it just kind of snuck up on us. We've been spending all this time together like we never had before, without pressures of work or anything else. I think we just started to click, and then last night, well…" James' voice trailed off.

"You don't have to give me any of the details, James," I answered.

"Shannon is quite a woman," James added. "She's smart, funny, a great athlete, and someone I like being around."

"I'm glad you two have hit it off, James. I really am," I answered, patting him on the shoulder.

"Do you need a hand with that stuff?" I pointed to the pile of items under his arm.

"Oh, that would be great, thanks." James passed me the bag and other items he had lost his grip on and then used his now-free hand to keep his towel in place.

"Where am I bringing these things?" I asked him.

"Shannon is up by the pool," James answered. "I'm just going to go back to my room for a second."

"What do you need? Maybe I can help you."

"No thanks, boss," he said with a smile. "I… well I just need to put a bathing suit on."

"Gotcha," I answered as I turned towards the stairs to head up to the pool.

When I got to the pool area and opened the door, I could see Shannon sitting in one of the deck chairs. The lights were turned down low but still on, and the lights in the pool were on as well to create a romantic atmosphere.

The pool door swished closed behind me as I walked in.

"Oh good, you're back," Shannon spoke without turning around. "I was starting to miss you."

I walked up quietly behind her and passed her bag around to her.

"I've been missing you, too," I said softly.

Shannon gasped and practically jumped out of her chair, knocking her bag over.

"Damian!" she said loudly. "I didn't know you were back. I thought you were..."

"Thought I was who?" I stood smiling at her as she blushed.

Shannon was at a loss for words, something that was unusual for her.

"How was your night?" she said to me, trying to change the subject quickly as she picked up her belongings.

"No complaints. What about yours?"

Shannon stood up and looked at me, seeming flustered again.

"It was fine," she answered quickly. "We had a nice time."

"So, I heard."
"What… what did James tell you?"

"He really didn't have to say too much since I saw him walking out of your room with a towel wrapped around his waist and nothing else on."

Shannon sat down on the lounge chair, shaking her head.

"Damian," she began. "I… I didn't plan anything like this, and you know I would never do anything that would get in the way of my job. Spending time with James, getting to know him and seeing how much we enjoy each other's company, well it just happened. I'll understand if you think it's a bad idea or if you want me to resign…"

"Shannon, hold on," I interrupted. "You're the best assistant I have ever had. You are the right person for this job. You're allowed to have a personal life outside of work you know. In fact, I encourage it. You have always spent way too much time wrapped up in doing your job. Don't worry about it."

Shannon breathed a big sigh of relief.

"I have been so worried about how you would react. Even after we…" Shannon stopped herself from talking too much about the previous night. "Well, I told James that maybe it wasn't a good idea since we work so closely together all the time. He managed to talk me out of it." Shannon flashed a bit of a smile as she said this.

"I'm sure everything will be fine," I told her. "I hope this makes you happy."

"It does, Damian, more than I have been in a long time. Thanks for giving me the chance to be here, and to let me see what I have been missing out on."
Shannon stepped over and gave me a big hug, pressing her body to mine. I hugged her back and gave her a quick peck on the cheek.

I heard the door slam shut and looked up, still holding Shannon in our embrace. There stood Kelly, looking at the two of us standing there hugging, with a shocked and angry look on her face that slowly turned to a pained one.

"Kelly… what are you doing…"

"Don't Damian," she said scornfully. "Just don't say anything. I see how things are." She held a piece of paper up in her hand, turned on her heels and stormed out.

"Wait!" I shouted and ran after her.

19

Kelly

I moved quickly out of the house, up the driveway and to the boardwalk without pausing or even looking back. All I could hear was a pounding in my ears and head, and I could feel my body getting hotter and hotter with each stride I took. It was bad enough to see that letter from Damian's company this morning but watching him embrace some other woman crushed me. I didn't know what to think at this moment; I just knew I had to be away from him.

I took long, fast steps, and felt my feet pound on the wooden planks beneath me, stomping like I was going to push right through them and have the boardwalk and the beach just swallow me up so I could disappear. Faintly in the background, I thought I heard Damian's voice call to me, far away at first, but getting closer. I refused to acknowledge it though and just made my way back towards the bakery.

When I got back to the bakery, Mom and Alex were behind the counters as they helped some early customers. I had flung the door open with such force that it bounced on its hinges and then slammed closed. The crash startled everyone in the shop. All heads lifted and spun towards me, but I just ignored them and stormed towards the counter, tossing the opening back so I could get into the kitchen, away from everyone.

I pushed through the swinging doors, and they rattled against the walls behind them. Jodie looked up quickly from the counter where she was working on icing some cinnamon buns. She saw the pain in my face and eyes and came over to me.

"What's wrong?" she said to me.

All the emotion that had built up inside me started to spill out.

"I went there… to his house… and… and" the words would not escape of my mouth without being surrounded by tears and a loss of breath.

"Kelly, calm down," Jodie said, as she led me over to a stool to sit down.

Just as I sat down, there was a bit of a commotion out in the shop. Damian's voice was distinctly in the shop, and he tried to find out where I was and what had happened. Within seconds, he had come through the kitchen doors and stood across the room from Jodie and me.

Damian's forehead was covered with sweat, and he worked to catch his breath as he looked over at us.

"Get out, Damian," I uttered, looking down at the floor. I knew if I had looked at him, I wouldn't be able to control myself.

"Jodie, can you give us a minute, please?" Damian panted, his hands on his hips.

Jodie went to leave the kitchen, and I grabbed her arm tightly.

"Don't go," I said quietly. "She's not going anywhere. We have nothing to talk about," I said more loudly to Damian.

"Kelly, what the hell is going on? You burst into the house, don't say anything, and then run out right away. What's wrong?"

"What's wrong?" I looked over at Jodi and let out a crazy laugh. "He wants to know what's wrong, Jodie. Like he has no idea what's going on."

I stood up quickly from the stool, pushing it to the side and walked right up to Damian, getting right in his face.

"What's wrong is you used me. You toyed with me for a few days while you had your people back in New York working on things the whole time, didn't you? Then once everything was done and you got what you wanted, you could celebrate with your girlfriend with a nice swim."

"What are you talking about?" Damian said to me.

"First we get this nice letter in the mail telling me I have to close the bakery and vacate because your company has bought up the whole strip so you can build some monstrosity office building or whatever else you feel like having with a view of the ocean. To top things off, you go back to your house after spending the night with me to whoever it is that's at your house so that you can have a good laugh at my expense."

Damian looked at Jodi and then looked at me. I was sure he could see my body as it trembled as I held the letter tightly in my right hand.

"What letter? I didn't buy anything," he professed.

"You must think I'm really ignorant, Damian. Just some small-town girl that will swoon over you and your money, get taken in by you, and then just roll over and go away. You can save the act for your bimbos back in New York. God, I can't believe I fell for this, and for... for you."

I turned away from Damian and went back towards Jodie. Tears were welling in my eyes, and my face felt hot from yelling. Jodie put her arms around me and held me as I cried louder.

I could hear Damian as he took a few steps across the room to come towards us.

"Don't!" I yelled.

"Damian, maybe you had better go," Jodie said strongly as she held me.

"I'm not sure what is going on here or what happened, but I am going to find out and come back," Damian said calmly.

"Don't bother," I said curtly. I turned to look directly at Damian. "You got what you wanted. You got the property, got to have some fun, and pulled one over on me. That should be enough for you. Get out. This is still my place, for now."

"Kelly, please..." Damian took two more steps closer to me and put his hand on my arm. I wrenched my hand away as quickly as I could.

"GET OUT!" I screamed. "You've fucked up my life enough, haven't you?"

Damian shook his head and shuffled out of the kitchen. I turned back to Jodie and sobbed loudly as she held me again.

No sooner had Damian left than Mom and Alex came into the kitchen to see what was going on. Everyone peppered me with questions, asking what happened, why I was so upset and so on. I explained what I saw when I entered Damian's house, with his arms wrapped around this woman in her bathing suit, smiling and laughing like they didn't have a care in the world.

"What a dick," Alex said in disgust.

"Alex, please go back out and watch the shop," Mom said to her.

"Why can't I stay? I'm part of this too," Alex complained.

"Because we have customers out there that need help," Jodie said, taking charge.

"Did he say anything about the letter?" Mom asked.

"I never even got the chance to ask him," I said. I dried my eyes with a paper towel that Jodie had handed to me. "As soon as I saw them together I turned around and left."

"Kelly, are you sure about what you saw?" Mom said to me.

"What is that supposed to mean? How else can I take that, Mom? He was hugging some woman dressed in a wet bikini in his house early in the morning. How am I supposed to react?"

"All I'm saying is that there may be more to it than what you saw. After meeting Damian and what you have said about him, it's just hard to believe that he would be like that."

"Mom, I know you always want to believe the best in people, but there are lots of assholes out there just looking to take advantage of people like you and me. I think he had you fooled… and he had me fooled too." I started crying again and felt Mom pat me on the back as Jodie held me once more.

Mom left the kitchen to go out to the shop, leaving me alone with Jodie.

"Jodie, I can't deal with this, I just can't. It feels like everything is crashing down right now."

"I know, Kelly," Jodie said as she consoled me. "We'll figure all this out. There has to be something we can do that can save the bakery."

The bakery was certainly a primary concern of mine, but there was so much more that tore me up inside. I thought I had found someone I could be with, enjoy, and most of all, trust. Now all of that disappeared in a matter of minutes, and I was left with nothing.

20

Damian

I walked slowly back towards my house, barely even noticing anyone along the way as I tried to figure out what was going on. Kelly didn't even give me the chance to find out facts about whatever letter she was talking about, and apparently when she saw me hugging Shannon, it was just the icing on the cake. I had to get the opportunity to talk to her more about what she saw, but she was not going to let me do it when she was as distraught as she was.

I tried to run through my head just what she could be talking about and how things got dismantled so quickly, and by the time I reached the house, I knew I had to start sorting through what facts I did know.

I walked through the door and lumbered up the stairs, lost in my thoughts. I went right past James on the second floor as he was coming out of the pool area.

"Everything okay, Boss?" he asked me.

"No… no, it's not."

I got up to the top floor and sat down on the couch, pondering everything that Kelly had said. James and Shannon both appeared, wrapped in towels from their swim.

"Damian, what's going on?" Shannon asked.

"That was Kelly in the house before. She's very upset. Something about a letter she got from our company saying we had bought the property on the boardwalk and were evicting her and the other businesses. Then she saw me hugging you, and I think the combination of the two was more than she could take."

"What property? I don't know about us buying anything," Shannon said with a confused look on her face. "Did you tell her who I was, or why we were hugging?"

"I never even got the chance to get a word in edgewise. Every time I tried to say something, she cut me off, and it just made things worse. I have to find out what is going on so I can straighten this mess out."

I grabbed my cell phone out of my pocket and tried to call Paul at the office. His cell phone went right to voicemail, and I left him a message to call me back right away. I then tried his office phone and got his assistant, Miranda, on the phone.

"Miranda, it's Damian. Is Paul in his office? I need to speak with him right away."

Miranda could sense the urgency in my voice.

"No Mr. Woods, he's not. He took today off to relax. He said something about you telling him to relax more, and then after this big deal he wanted to celebrate."

"What big deal?" I raised my voice more than I normally would have, and I think it shocked Miranda on the other end.

"The purchase that he... he just closed on. The property in Delaware for the new office. He said it was just what you would have wanted and that he got it for a great deal."

I sighed deeply, trying to hold back my anger.

"Miranda, do you have copies of the paperwork of the deal? I would like to see it."

"Yes, I have the hard copies here, but the electronic ones are only on Paul's laptop, and he has that with him."

"Scan the pages in and send them to my email," I said gruffly. "And do all you can to get a hold of Paul. As soon as you reach him, tell him to call me, or you call me and let me know what's going on."

"Did I... did I do something wrong, Mr. Woods?" Miranda said with hesitation.

"No," I told her. I tried to regain my composure as best as I could. "You didn't do anything. Thanks for your help, Miranda." I hung up the phone abruptly and sat down on the couch.

"Paul closed some deal this week for the property. Miranda is sending me the paperwork so I can see what this is all about."

"Can he really do that without getting your approval first?" James asked me.

"He can, but he's supposed to let me know about it before he goes ahead with anything like that."

Shannon sat on the couch next to me.

"He has been trying to reach you for days," Shannon said quietly.

"I know, but he also knew that this was time away from work for me. He couldn't wait to try to do this deal until after my vacation was done so I could say no? What was the big rush to do this? I don't get it. And now things are royally screwed up with Kelly. She thinks this was all my doing like it was some devious plan on my part to get the property."

I got up and paced around the room a bit, trying to figure out what I could do to convince Kelly that this wasn't any of my doing. Accomplishing that seemed impossible at this point, especially since it was my company that did all this, and she did see me with Shannon without knowing who she was or why she was in my house so early in the morning.

I heard my email ding at the arrival of a new message and saw it was the scanned files from Miranda. I opened them quickly and began to study them, looking over the contract and then the sample of the letter that was sent to all the business owners that were being forced out of their locations so quickly. After reading everything I sat back on the couch, resting my head on the back cushion and staring up at the ceiling, trying to decide my next move.

"How's it look?" Shannon asked me, handing me a cup of coffee that she had just made.

"It seems pretty cut and dry as far as a real estate deal goes. There's nothing special about it. It's a good chunk of that area of the boardwalk. It's going to force out about a dozen or so businesses. There's a cash incentive there for businesses to vacate quickly that some may have taken advantage of already. I don't know how he managed to get this done so fast. It's not like he knew about the house I had down here already or my plans, and we've only been here for a few days. Something's not right about all this."

I closed my laptop and tossed it into my briefcase, and then picked up my phone and tried to reach Paul again, without any luck. I slammed my phone down on the table in disgust. Shannon came over and put her hand on my shoulder.

"What can we do to help?"

"At this point, I don't know what anyone can do. The contracts have been signed and filed. Technically, the business owns the property right now, and with people already taking the incentive cash, I don't see a clear way out of all this. No wonder Kelly was so mad. God, she must really hate me right now, and I can't say I blame her."

The sun was up and shone brightly now, and I looked out the windows, out over the ocean, and tried to imagine what had been running through Kelly's head after we had spent the past few days together. The time I had spent with her was better than any I had spent with anyone else, and to see all that tossed away so suddenly was devastating to me. I had to do whatever I could to try to make things right, to see what had truly occurred. Even when I ran over the scenarios myself, I didn't see how to make things better.

I walked over to the table, grabbed my briefcase and started to make my way down the stairs.

"Where are you going?" Shannon yelled.

"I have to get back to New York," I replied as I made my way down towards the garage. "I'm taking the Mustang. If you find out anything from Paul or hear from him, get in touch with me right away."

"Boss, why don't you let me drive you?" James said as he followed me down the stairs. "Maybe you aren't in the best state of mind to drive yourself right now."

"I appreciate the offer, James, but I can handle it. I'll be careful, I promise."

I took a quick look at my watch and saw it was almost eight in the morning. I knew if I left right now, I could be in New York by one or two, giving me plenty of time to get to the office before everyone was gone for the day.

I pulled the Mustang out of the garage and headed out towards Route 1 as fast as I could. I hoped to get this taken care of and get back to talk to Kelly, if she would let me, before things went too far to save.

21

Kelly

Usually, the bakery was my happy place, the place I could retreat to that was my domain. I could get lost in what I was doing, be creative, and know that I owned what was happening. After everything that went down in the morning, I no longer felt that way. Every time I looked up or tried to concentrate on work, the thoughts would just flash across my mind about how Damian had let me down, betrayed me, taken all I had worked for in one fell swoop. To make things worse, he had captured my heart and then broken it quickly, and I wasn't sure how I would recover from either of these devastations.

My family did their best to try to make things better for me. They encouraged me to leave the bakery, go home and figure things out. Honestly, I always did my best thinking when I was working so I just kept at it. I voraciously dove into the dough, and made tray after tray of cookies and pastries, crafted pie dough and even made some breads just so I could keep my hands and my mind busy working on something else, anything else but what had happened.

By the time we got close to the end of the day, my body and mind were spent. I went out to the storefront and slumped into one of the chairs, causing a puff of flour to rise off my covered apron. I leaned my head against the wall and covered my face with a sack towel as I closed my eyes. I could hear Alex whisper to my mother, and then the clang of Alex dropping some of the empty trays from the display cases onto the floor. I heard scurrying about and then the kitchen door whooshing open and closed, and the slow, shuffling feet of my mother as she came over and sat in the chair across from me. The familiar sound of a coffee mug sliding across the table was in front of me, and as I peeled the towel from the front of my eyes, I could smell the rich aroma of what Mom had just brewed for me.

I tossed the towel onto the table and picked up the mug, inhaling the smell so it could perk me up a bit before I took a sip.

"We were busy today," Mom noted, trying to skirt around the real issues that were in front of me. I just nodded to her as I sipped more coffee.

"Kelly," Mom started, "I know you feel like you got body slammed today by all this. I wish I could do something to take what you are going through away from you. I always hate when one of you is struggling or hurt. I know it sounds cliché, but you will get through this – WE will get through this."

"That's easy to say, Mom. It's a lot harder to do. We're losing everything, all we worked so hard far, all the money we sunk into this place to get started. We put our souls into this place, and one piece of paper is going to take it all away."

"Maybe," Mom said softly, "Maybe we should just take his money. To hell with him and take the buyout. We can start over somewhere else in town. We have a good core of local customers. People will support you, Kelly, you know they will."

"Even if we took his money it wouldn't be enough to get started over at a new location. We would have to find a spot, get equipment, and spend months getting set up again. Think of all we would lose in that time. By then, summer is over, all the tourists are gone, and a huge chunk of our business with it. And we'll never find a spot as good as this one, right on the boardwalk with lots of foot traffic. If we're off in town somewhere, we get fewer people coming by and less business. I don't see how we can make it work."

I took another sip of coffee and then gripped the towel in my hand, squeezing. I was frustrated, angry, and sad all at the same time. I had let myself trust again, let myself get close to someone – let myself fall in love – and it all came back to bite me. Nothing seemed fair about any of it. I put the towel back over my eyes to cover the sting of the tears that were forming in my eyes. I heard myself start to sniffle, and my mother reached over and gently took my hand in hers while I cried.

The bakery front door opened as the bells on it lightly jingled. Mom's chair creaked as she pivoted to look back at whoever had entered, and she stood up to go behind the counter.

"I'm afraid there's not much left," Mom said to the patrons. "It's pretty near to closing time."

"I'm actually here to see Kelly... Kelly Barton," a woman's voice stated.

I removed the towel from my face, wiping my eyes as I did, and looked at the woman standing in front of me. It was the person I saw in the bathing suit hugging Damian. She looked over at me and turned to face me.

"I'm Shannon," she said to me. "I think we need to talk about a few things."

"I really have nothing to say to you," I said gruffly. I stood up and moved away from her to go back to the kitchen.

"Kelly, wait!" I heard a man's voice yell. I looked back and saw James just inside the door. "There are a lot of things you're missing to all this. Let us at least fill you in, and then you can decide what to do, okay? Please?"

I sat back down and crossed my arms over my chest. "Go ahead," I replied. "Tell me about how Damian screwed me out of my business, and about how he was holding..." I was tearing up again as I spoke. "Holding you in his arms. I saw you with him. There's nothing you can say that will change what I saw."

Shannon sat down across from me.

"Yes, you saw him hugging me, but you don't know why he was doing that," she explained. "I'm Damian's personal assistant..."

"I bet you are," I said sarcastically.

"Kelly, let her explain," Mom interrupted. "Maybe there's more to this."

"Sure, maybe they want the keys to my house too since they are taking everything else away."

"Kelly, please," Shannon said to me. I saw she was trying to hold her composure, "I have worked for Damian for a few years now. There is nothing romantic at all between us. There never has been. He was hugging me... well... because James and I had just told him that we are involved with each other."

James came over and put his hand on Shannon's shoulder.

"It's true, Kelly," James said to me. "I know it looks like horrible timing and coincidences, but you have to believe me.

Damian didn't do anything and has nothing going on with Shannon."

"Then how come I hadn't seen her at the house?" I asked, trying to figure all this out. "I saw you plenty of times, James, but I never saw her there."

"I can't explain it," Shannon told me. "Like James said, it's just timing. I have been there the whole time James and Damian have been there. Please, I'm telling you the truth. Damian... he's not the type of guy who would do that... see multiple women, or cheat on someone that he really cares about."

I didn't know what to believe at this point. Were they just giving me a story at Damian's urging to smooth things over? Or was it the truth and was a series of bad coincidences that led to a misunderstanding? And did Damian really care about me the way I felt about him? It was all very confusing.

"Even if what you say is true, that doesn't change the fact about your business forcing me out. The letter is pretty cut and dry about that."

"I know," Shannon said to me. "Damian didn't have anything to do with that. His lawyer has the power to make deals and acquisitions on behalf of the business. Damian came down here to get away from the business for a bit. He hasn't answered any phone calls, emails, messages or anything since he has been here. Honestly, he has spent more time with you than doing anything else. What happened with the buyout was out of his hands. I don't have all the details yet, but I am working on getting them. And Damian took off to go back to New York to find out the truth. He's probably just about there already. I've tried calling him, but he's not answering his phone."

"Why… why should I believe any of this?" I said softly.

"Because it's the truth, Kelly," James said to me. "Look, I know you're probably confused about all this. Hell, I'm still confused about the business end of it, but I know one thing for certain – Damian wouldn't do anything that would hurt you in any way. "

I stood up and took my apron off and walked over to Mom.

"What do you think, Mom?" I said quietly. I needed her input now more than ever.

Mom looked me straight in the eyes and gave me her gentle smile. She took my hands in hers.

"It doesn't matter what I think right now, Kelly. This is all about you. I will say, though, that if it were me, I would want to hear what Damian has to say for himself. You need to have a heart-to-heart with him, so you know what happened, how he feels, and how you feel."

I hugged Mom tightly, and after we broke the hug, I turned and stared at James and Shannon.

"Okay," I said, wiping my eyes one last time. "If this is true, then I need to go to New York."

Everyone in the room said "What?" at the same time, including Jodie and Alex, who had been listening just inside the kitchen doors.

"I need to talk to Damian, face to face. I have to hear it from him about everything – the business deal, what I saw, and how he feels. It's the only way I am going to be able to decide what the truth is."

"You're going to drive your crappy old pickup up there?" Jodie asked. "You haven't driven that thing more than five miles in years. Who knows how it will be?"

"I'll take you," James stated. "We can take the Lexus, and I'll drive you up there. It's the fastest way to get there."

"I can't ask you to do that," I told James.

"It's fine, I do it all the time," James told me. "Besides, I know where to go and the best way to get there in a quicker time. Let me take care of it."

James wasn't going to take no for an answer, so I nodded in agreement. Alex had darted into the kitchen to grab my bag. James leaned over and gave Shannon a kiss before we left, and I could see the smile creep across her face as he did. They certainly looked as if they were with each other.

There is more to this that I need to know, I thought to myself.

James held up his keys and opened the bakery door for me, and I walked out onto the boardwalk to head towards Damian's house where the car was.

I didn't say anything to James the whole walk to the house. I kept myself focused on trying to figure out what I was going to say and do once I got to New York, and what kind of answers I was going to get from Damian.

22

Damian

I sped the Mustang all along Route 1 and across the Delaware Memorial Bridge, weaving in and out of traffic like I never had before. I didn't even care if the police were going to stop me for speeding at this point; I just needed to get back to the city, confront Paul, and figure out what was done and if there was a way to undo it. At least if I could fix this part of the problem then maybe I could explain it all to Kelly and get her to see everything that was going on.

Traffic on the New Jersey Turnpike naturally slowed me down. I had managed to reach the Turnpike by about noon, and I thought I could get to the office in plenty of time, but between a glut of traffic and then a jackknifed tractor-trailer near Exit 9 that brought everyone to a halt, I stewed about the situation and how everything had gone from wonderful to horrible in the span of about ten minutes. I repeatedly tried to call Paul on his cell phone or at the office, but I couldn't get through to him.

By the time traffic got moving again and I crept by the accident site, it was closing in on in almost four, and I was getting worried that it was taking me too long to get to the city. I felt my foot getting heavier on the gas as I passed car after car like they were standing still. All the traffic became just a blur to me before I got to my exit and made my way through the Lincoln Tunnel and into the city.

As I sat impatiently in traffic in the city, the ringing of my cell phone jolted my mind away from Kelly. I pressed the answer button on the steering wheel and heard that it was Miranda.

"Mr. Woods, Paul just called me and told me he is on his way to the office. I told him you were trying to get in touch with him, and it was urgent, but... well, he didn't seem too responsive."

"What do you mean he wasn't too responsive?"

"It sounded like... I don't want to say anything bad about him..." Miranda said with hesitation.

"Miranda, just tell me what's going on." There was a clear tone of aggravation in my voice.

"I think he's been drinking. There was a lot of noise in the background, so I'm not sure where he was, but he sounded like he was slurring his words."

"Miranda, if he gets to the office before I do, just make sure he stays in his office. I should be there in about twenty minutes or so."

"You're in the city?" she said with a worried lilt to her voice. "Yes, I'll do what I can to keep him there."

"Do more than what you can, Miranda. If you have to call security to hold him in there, then do it."

Miranda was quiet for a moment before she answered me. I'm sure she had never heard me this angry and wasn't sure if I really meant it about security, but I certainly did.

"Yes, Mr. Woods," she said quietly.

I hung up the phone and began tapping my palms on the steering wheel, trying to urge the traffic to move along faster so I could get to our building. My phone rang a couple of times, and I could see it was Shannon trying to reach me, but I was too busy concentrating on this problem to deal with whatever might be going on in Delaware on her end.

One catastrophe at a time, I told myself as I could finally see our building up ahead.

I moved quickly into the underground parking garage and pulled up to the security gate. Walter, one of our older security guards, was operating the booth and peered over at me, unaccustomed to seeing me driving and in a Mustang.

"Mr. Woods?" he said with surprise. "I thought you were away on vacation. Nice car," he said, admiring the vehicle.

"Thanks, Walter, I said hurriedly. "Walter, has Paul Austin come through yet?"

"Yes, he just entered about ten minutes ago. He practically drove through the gate. Is everything okay?"

"I hope so," I said to Walter as I the gate rose and I drove off to get to my parking spot.

One of the perks of being the boss is having a private spot right near a private elevator so that I could get up to our floor quickly. I parked the car and went straight to the elevator, swiping my security card so the doors would open. I tapped my foot all the way up to our floor, trying not to pay attention to the music coming out over the speakers so I could focus on what I was going to say to Paul.

The elevator opened and was right near my office. Paul's office was just down the hall to the left, and I quickly paced my way over there. A few heads turned when they saw me walking down the hall, wearing a pair of shorts and sneakers. I turned right and saw Miranda sitting at her desk. She had a little bit of a panicked look on her face.

"Is he in there?" I asked her.

"He is Mr. Woods but..."

Before Miranda could say anything else, I breezed past her and opened the door to Paul's office. There was Paul, with his feet up on his desk, a glass in his hand that looked like it was filled with booze. Music blared in his office, and when I looked to his left, I could see two women sitting on the leather couch, both in various stages of undress, smiling and laughing. Paul recognized it was me in his office and smiled at me.

"Damian!" he yelled, holding up his glass to me. "What are you doing back? I thought you were on vacation."

Paul spun his chair around and got to his feet, wobbling a bit as he did. He walked over to the couch and held his hands out to the ladies that were there, helping them to their feet.

"Damian, this is Lola and Brianna. They were celebrating with me last night, and I thought I would bring them in to keep the party going. We were just playing a little game of Truth or Dare. Care to join us?'

"No, thanks." I peered at Paul and saw him put his arm around the waist of one of the girls, pulling her to him and planting a kiss on her neck.

"Ladies, you need to leave... now," I ordered.

"Oh, come on, Damian. We're just having some fun. Lola there is a real spitfire if you're interested, but Brianna here is mine today."

"The party is over, Paul. I need to speak with you about business matters, alone." I walked over to the office door and held it open so the ladies could exit. Both girls picked up the purses from the table, and Brianna went over and gave Paul a kiss on the cheek.

"Just wait for me outside, honey," Paul said to her. "This won't take long, and then we can get back to things."

The girls walked past me, and I shut the door as they went out. Paul had already gone back behind his desk and picked up his glass. He reached down and picked up the bottle of scotch and poured himself more so that it overflowed the top of the glass.

"Paul, what the hell are you doing?" I barked.

"What? You told me to relax and have some fun, so that's what I've been doing. You were right Damian; I've been missing out on a lot of life. It's been a blast the last few days, one party after another. Can I pour you a drink?"

I sat down in the chair across from Paul's desk, trying to maintain my composure, but it was getting more difficult for me to do.

"Paul, I need you to focus for a few minutes so you can tell me about this business deal you made this week."

Paul gazed at me, his pupils wide and dilated. I couldn't tell if he was just drunk, on something, or some combination of the two.

"What business deal? I do deals all the time Damian. You'll have to be more specific."

"The one in Delaware, on the boardwalk. What did you do?"
"Oh that one," he said as he shuffled paperwork and folders on his desk that were piled up.

"That was the one I am celebrating the most," he said proudly. "I figured since you said you wanted to spend time down there and had a house there now that it made sense to have some office space there too. I looked around and saw that this space was close to your house, contacted the company that owns the land, and made them an offer. They jumped at the first one I gave them. It probably saved us millions. It was a great score and making the arrangements to turn it all into office space, well that was a masterpiece as well. It took greasing a few palms along the way, but money opens a lot of doors. But I don't have to tell you that."

Paul smiled at me and drank some more.

"What do you mean greased some palms?"

"Come on, Damian, don't be naïve. You think these real estate transactions happen without any backroom deals? I do this stuff all the time. Everyone always wants an extra piece of pie for these things to happen. I just quietly make some "donations" or whatever to help move things along. What are you all upset about? This was a great deal, and now we can have an office on the beach. Think of the marketing we can do. We'll have enough space to have a research area where we can do stuff and have the ocean right there. This is big for us. I thought you would be happy about it."

"Your deal is putting a lot of businesses down there out. You sent letters evicting people already. You should have at least run this by me before you closed it all so quickly. And the fact that you have been doing things illegally to get it done, well that's another problem. What were you thinking?"

"I thought that this was a good opportunity and that you told me not to contact you," Paul told me. I could see he was starting to get defensive now. "I tried to reach you a few times, but you and Shannon ignored my calls, so I just went ahead with it. Why are you taking this so personally? So, we close a t-shirt shop, surf shop and a bakery and some other places. Big deal."

"I have... friends that the deal is affecting, closing their business. They came to me, and I knew nothing about it." I was trying to be delicate about the situation, but the more we talked about this, the more anger welled up inside me.

"Hey, we offered everyone a buyout to move. They could just take the money and go. A couple of places already did. It will save us a ton in trying to get them out of there so we can start on demolition. Which business came to you? I'm sure I can deal with them."

Paul shuffled some papers, looking at information about the deal. "Was it the bakery?" Paul held up a file folder in his hand and opened it up.

"Yes, it was the bakery, in fact," I said to him.

"Hmmm," he mused as he looked at the file. "Family owned business for a few years. All women I see. Kelly Barton, she's the owner listed. I did some background info on everyone involved in case I needed to do some work." He held up another folder and opened it. This one had pictures of Kelly and her family, and what I assumed was background information on her.

"Wow, she looks cute," Paul said with a smirk. "Is she the 'friend' you were talking about? I can see why you would want to keep her happy. Don't worry, I'll up the offer to her to give her some extra cash to vacate. I'm sure she'll jump at it. She doesn't seem to have much going for her. It's not like she has the means to fight us on anything."

Paul closed the folder and started drinking again.

"Okay, I've had enough of this," I said standing up. "How can we undo this?"

"Undo it?' Paul said with a laugh. "Damian, you can't undo stuff like this. I signed contracts, money has already changed hands. It's a done deal. We own the property. Don't be ridiculous. You don't want an office there? Fine. I'll turn around and sell the property to someone else. We'll make a ton of money. Either way works for me. Don't get yourself all worked up over this because some woman you're crushing on comes crying to you. Go back to Delaware, give her a tumble, throw some money at her, and it will be done, and you'll feel better."

"I never realized what a complete dick you are, Paul," I said to him.

"Hey, I'm the dick that has helped you along the way to get richer. You should be thanking me instead of giving me a hard time."

You're right, Paul," I told him. "I should be thanking you for this conversation because it has made me see what's been going on."

I walked over to the office door and opened it a bit.

"Miranda, call security up here," I said to her and closed the door again.

"What do you want security for?" Paul said, finishing his drink.

"To escort you out of the building. You're fired, Paul. I'll give you time to collect your personal belongings, and then security will escort you out. Anything business related stays here – your computer, your files, business information, all of it. If you take one piece of paper, one pencil that doesn't belong to you, I'll have the police at your home."

"You're firing me over this? For a woman?" Paul stood up and walked over to stand in front of me. We were about the same height, and I looked him right in the eyes.

"No, not just over a woman, Paul. I can come up with about six reasons to do it outside of her. Be grateful that I am not turning you in to the Bar Association, the government, or the police. Who knows how long it is going to take to fix what you have been doing around here. Pack up and leave or things will get much worse for you."

Security came into Paul's office just as Paul was starting to make a threatening move towards me. The officers rushed over, with one taking Paul by the arm and the other standing between him and me.

"Are you okay, Mr. Woods?" the one guard asked me.

"I'm fine," I said to him. "Stay with Mr. Austin while he collects his personal belongings and then escort him from the building. Make sure to get his credentials, his pass keys, and anything else that belongs to us. Goodbye, Paul."

I walked towards the office door as Paul shouted, "Fuck you, Damian!"

Miranda was standing up at her desk, looking shocked.
"Mr. Woods, what's going on? What's happening with Paul?" she asked worriedly.

"Paul's gone," I told her, looking at her. "Don't let him have anything from your desk or out here, Miranda. That's all corporate property."

"What's... what is going to happen to me?" Miranda asked.

"Miranda, I am going to assume that you didn't have anything to do with any of the illegal activities Paul may have been engaged in. You'll have to meet with HR and security to discuss everything. We should be able to move you to another area. We'll work it out."

"Illegal activities?" Miranda gasped. "Mr. Woods, I swear, I haven't done anything, really."

"Good," I said to her. "I'm going to my office. I need to contact HR and the Board of Directors about all this and try to straighten out some other things. If security needs me for anything, they can come to get me."

I went back towards my office with people looking at me as they could hear shouting come from Paul's office. I opened my office door and went behind my desk, flipping my computer open to get it turned on. I would have to call down to HR to let them know what had happened, and then talk to the Board and try to explain this mess so we could work on getting another attorney in place quickly.

The mess looked like it was just getting bigger instead of under control, and I still needed to figure out a way to try to fix the boardwalk issues and do something about Kelly. I spun around in my chair to look out over the water as I dialed HR on my desk phone. I spotted some thick, dark clouds starting to move towards the city. A thunderstorm was brewing for sure around here.

23

———————————

Kelly

The ride towards New York was stressful from the moment I sat down in the car with James. I think we drove an hour or two in complete silence, with James working his way up towards the bridge in record time. There were times I felt myself holding on to the strap hanging above the door or the door itself because I wasn't sure if we were going to make it between cars. I gave him a few glances occasionally when things were particularly hairy, and he just smiled at me before we eventually reached the bridge.

"You know," James said, breaking the silence, "if you thought that was scary, wait until we get further up the Turnpike towards the city."

"Great, "I said as I turned back towards the window so I wouldn't have to see what James was doing.

"Kelly, can I just say one thing about Damian?" James asked me.

I turned towards him and just looked at him, giving silent assent.

"Damian is a good man," James began. "He's not the type of person who is going try to manipulate someone or a situation just for financial gain. I've met wealthy people like him since I started working for him, and he stands out among them. Most of these guys just like to flaunt their money so that people notice them and how rich they are. Even when they think they are doing something nice like donating to charity, they do it so they get their name in the paper and good press. Damian isn't like that. He genuinely wants to do what is right and help. He may not be close to many people, but to those that get close to him, he cares for them. He's not just the best boss I have ever had. He's the best person that I have known. When I say I know he didn't have anything to do with this, I am confident about it."

"I hope you're right James, for both our sakes," I said as I leaned my head against the cool glass of the window.

A few smatterings of rain fell against the windows, and there was a low rumble of thunder as rain was starting to come upon us.

"If the rain gets heavy it might slow us down some," James added. "Do you want me to call the office and see if he is there? Maybe we can let him know we're coming."

"No, it's fine," I said softly. "I don't want Damian to know we are on the way there. Besides, I'm still trying to figure out just what I am going to say to him, and how I'll react to what he has to say to me. It's all very confusing."

We went back to our silence in the car and got closer and closer to New York City. I hadn't set foot in New York City since I went back to Bethany Beach after the heartache I felt years ago. Just being in the city caused tension for me and I sat up straight in my seat the minute we headed to the tunnel. We even drove past the location of the restaurant I had worked in after culinary school, though I could see now that it had closed and turned into one of those casual dining places you see all over the place.

James made a series of lefts and rights so quickly it was hard for me to keep up with just where we were, and suddenly we were pulling into an underground parking garage. James pulled up to the security gate and flashed his work badge.

"Hey Jimmy," the guard said to him. "Sweet ride. Is this yours or does it belong to the boss?"

"It's Mr. Woods' car," James told him. "Have you seen him come in at all?"

"Sorry, I just came on a few minutes ago. I haven't seen him since I've been here."

The guard peered into the car and saw me sitting there.

"Jimmy, I need to see her ID before I can let you in," the guard told him.

"Eddie," James said to the guard, "we really need to get in and see if Mr. Woods is here. She's a friend of his; it's fine."

"Jimmy, you know the security rules," Eddie replied. "I could lose my job if something happens."

"James, it's not a problem…" I started as I began rummaging through my bag for my wallet.

"Stop," James told me. "Eddie, I'm vouching for her. That should be good enough for you. If anyone has a problem, they can come to see me. Now open the damn gate."

I am sure Eddie saw the same look on James' face that I did, and James didn't look like the kind of guy that you wanted to be around if he lost his cool. Eddie just nodded to him and pressed the button to raise the gate so that we could enter.

I heard the tires of our car squeal on the pavement as we moved off and into the parking garage. A few more quick turns, and we were at what looked like a private entrance. James pulled the car into one of the two parking spots that were here.

"Well, his car isn't here," James said as he parked. "But that doesn't mean he isn't here. His apartment is only a few blocks from here. He could've parked there and walked over to the office."

"Okay," I said, taking off my seatbelt. "Let's go see if he's there."

We got out of the car and went to the elevator entrance. The elevator only had one button in it to go up or down, which meant it only went to the floor where Damian wanted it to go. The doors closed silently, and I never felt the elevator move as we shot up towards the office floor. The doors slid open, and we were outside a couple of closed oak doors. There was a desk area to the left of the doors, and huge windows that looked out over the ocean.

James went over and knocked on the office doors, but there was no reply. He tried the handle, which was locked, and then used his badge to open the door. I peered in around James, but all we saw was an empty office, dimly lit by a single light that was on near one of the couches.

"Let me go check and see if anyone is here that may have seen him," James said to me as we walked out of Damian's office. "Just wait right here. I'll only be gone a minute."

I nodded, and James was off, looking to find someone that might still be at work. I moved to look out the large windows, and I could see the rain and storm over the water. Between the time of night it was turning and the storm, it was getting dark on the water, and the bright lights of the skyline were illuminating what was beneath. That nervous feeling was overcoming me once again as I worried about talking to Damian and getting the truth, whether I wanted to hear it or not.

There was a bit of commotion behind me as I could hear a man yelling some profanities, so I turned to see what was going on. There was a man in a rumpled suit, carrying a few boxes with a security guard walking next to him. The man was mumbling something to the guard as I watched. His gaze locked onto mine and he stopped what he was doing.

"It's you," he said as if he recognized me. "The bakery owner."

"Do I know you?" I asked with some hesitation in my voice.

"Sure you do," he spat at me. "I'm the one whose life you ruined. Because of you, I lost my job, my career, probably everything I had."

"I have no idea what you are talking about," I said to him, trying to sound strong. I was too afraid to move and was hoping the security guard would just hustle this guy out of here.

"Right, play all innocent," he said as he walked closer to me. "What, did Damian bring you up here with him so he could show you his fancy office, maybe take you back to his apartment? Trust me, sister, you may be able to get what you want by crying a few tears to him or showing him a good time with that body of yours, but you won't last. I'll make sure of that now."

I was very frightened, and this man had a crazed look in his eyes. I looked to the security guard, giving him a pleading look, and he finally stepped in.

"Let's go, Mr. Austin," the guard told him. "I wasn't supposed to let you back up here for more stuff. We need to get out of here."

"Just keep quiet, rent-a-cop," he said pushing the guard to the ground and the lunging towards me. I yelled as he pressed his body tightly against mine and against the window, so I had nowhere left to go.

"I can see why he likes you so much," the man whispered.

I could smell the heavy scent of alcohol on his breath as I tried to wriggle away from him. His hands, which had started on my hips, were now moving their way up my sides towards my breasts.

"Please, leave me alone," I said trying to get free from him. The security guard still lay on the ground, his head having bounced off the floor.

I saw the man's face coming in towards mine to try to kiss me, I turned my head and closed my eyes, and as I did this, I felt his head getting jerked back away from me, and he yelled. My eyes opened, and I saw James grabbing him by the hair and tossing him into a cubicle wall. His body slid down the wall in a heap.

"Are you alright?" James said to me.

I just nodded to him as he turned back around. There was Mr. Austin, on his knees, getting ready to stand up. Two more security guards came racing down the hall and grabbed him by the arms, holding him as he flailed his body. James took me by the arm as we walked over towards the guards.

"Get him out of here," James yelled to them.

Mr. Austin had some blood trickling down his forehead from where he had hit the cubicle wall. He looked at me with a dazed look before giving me a crooked smile. I looked him right in the eyes, smiled back at him, and gave him a swift kick to the groin. He yelped and fell to the floor again.

"Nicely done," James said as he ushered me back to the private elevator.

"Thank you for your help," I said to James, holding his arm. "Who was that?"

"Paul Austin, the corporate attorney, or former corporate attorney anyway," James said as he pressed the down button. "He's the guy who brokered the deal to buy part of the boardwalk. Damian came in, talked to him, found what he did, along with some other illegal stuff he's been doing I guess, and fired him."

I felt a bit of relief from learning that information. It did seem like Damian was on my side after all.

"So, where's Damian?" I asked as the elevator doors opened.

"No one knows for sure," James told me. "I talked to Miranda, Paul Austin's assistant. She said Damian was talking to HR and then the Board of Directors, but he left here just before we arrived. We can check his apartment."

We got back into the car and drove the few blocks over to a large skyscraper with more underground parking. Again, we went through security and another private elevator that brought us up to a penthouse apartment. The elevator opened right into the apartment, and it looked like one of those places you see in interior design magazines. The place was easily bigger than my tiny house, and that was only what I could see.

James dashed around, looking in different rooms, but there was no sign of Damian or that he had even been here. I saw James take his phone out of his pocket and make a call, but he hung up shortly after.

"He's not picking up," James muttered. "Let me see if Shannon has heard from him."

James dialed his phone again, and this time spent a few minutes talking. I fidgeted in place while he talked, seeing more of the room around me and feeling more out of my element with each passing second. Was I just deluding myself into thinking that Damian would be interested in someone like me, someone so obviously different from the lifestyle he leads?

"Shannon hasn't heard from him either, but she said she'll keep trying him," James told me." I followed him back to the elevator and down to where the car was parked.

"We can try a few of the places he normally goes for dinner or a drink," James offered. "He probably was hungry and wanted something."

"It's okay, James," I said resignedly to him. "If it's all the same to you, I would just like to go home."

"Are you sure? I can put you up in the guest room up here, or in one of the hotels around here so you can spend the night and then talk to him when he gets in. It's no trouble. I'm sure I can find…"

I interrupted James, looking at him tearfully.

"Please James. Please just take me back to Delaware."

"Sure," he told me.

We climbed back into the car and were off once again. The rain came down a little harder now, falling against the window and streaking the outside while my tears streaked my cheeks.

24

_____

Kelly

I had drifted off to sleep somewhere not long after we got our trip back to Delaware started. I was exhausted from all the events of the day, and sleeping was a good way for me to avoid having to talk any more about Damian with James, or to even think about Damian Woods. Or at least I thought it was a good way to forget about him. My dreams were naturally filled with thoughts of him, replaying the times we had spent together at the beach, our balloon ride, in his pool, and in his bed. Every moment seemed so right to me, it was difficult to see how it got all screwed up.

I woke when James was nudging me, and I pried my eyes open and saw we were in the driveway of Damian's house in Bethany. I blinked a few times to try to focus on the clock on the dashboard and saw it was just after three in the morning.

"I'm sorry," I said to James, "I guess I slept the entire way back."

"It's fine," he said to me. "You obviously needed it. I can give you a ride over to your house if you want. I was just going to run and check on Shannon and see if Damian was here while you were asleep. You're welcome to come in and just sleep here if you want."

"It's okay, James," I told him as I took off my seatbelt and stretched a bit. "I can walk from here. It will do me good to be out of the car for a while."

I stepped out of the car and felt the fine mist that was still coming down. The rain sent a brief chill through my body as I started to walk over to the driver's side. James reached into the car and handed me an umbrella.

"Here take this," he said. "At least you won't get soaked while you're walking."

Before I opened the umbrella, I gave James a big hug.

"Thank you so much for all your help," I said to him. "You went well above the call of duty. Shannon is lucky to have you."

"No trouble at all," he said to me as he patted my back. "You know, just because you didn't get to talk to him tonight doesn't mean this won't all work out. I'm sure he's working on something."

"I don't know, James. Maybe… maybe it just wasn't meant to be. There were just too many differences to fight through."

"If you really felt that way you would have given up already and not tried to track him down in New York," James said to me. "Go home, sleep on it, and see what the sunrise brings. Take care, Kelly."

James watched me as I walked up the driveway and out the street. I stood on the corner for a moment, looking at the quiet area, and decided that instead of going home I was going to the bakery. It was practically time for me to get there any way to start the next day of work. I could get a jump on things and get items started and think about something else besides Damian.

I walked to and climbed the steps to the boardwalk and began my trek towards the bakery. The boardwalk was silent and empty. With the rain, there weren't even any walkers, joggers, or fishermen out getting ready for the morning. All I could hear was the mist gently pattering on my umbrella, and the sound of the ocean waves as they moved on shore.

I made my way over to the shop and noticed that there were lights on inside. I peered through the front window and could see that the one light was on over the coffee machines and that the lights in the kitchen were on. I couldn't believe that Jodie or my Mom forgot to turn off the lights at closing time since it was such a part of the routine each day. Since I was at the front of the bakery, I took my keys out to just open the front door and shut the alarm off from this side instead of the kitchen. As I went to put my key in the lock, the door moved slightly, indicating it was already unlocked. There was no way they would forget to lock the front door, and no one ever came in this way when we always worked in the kitchen before opening.

I pulled my phone out of my pocket and got ready to dial 911, but I opened the front door first instead. I closed the door behind me quietly and took soft steps towards the counter so as not to startle anyone. A quick glance at the register showed it was still off and locked, so no one had tried to break into it (not that there was ever any cash in it anyway; that always went in the safe). I could hear moving around in the kitchen and the soft sound of music playing.

I pushed open the kitchen door and startled the person in the kitchen so that they dropped a bowl on the floor.

"Damian? What the hell are you doing here?" I asked.

"Well I was making a batch of biscuits for breakfast, but that's pretty much ruined now," he said as he bent down and picked up the bowl and the dough that had fallen on the floor.

"Why are you in my kitchen? I thought you were in New York. How did you get in here?"

"I do own the building now," he said to me. "Getting keys was just a formality."

"So that's how you want to end this?" I growled. "Fine, take it," I said as I tossed my keys at him and marched out the kitchen doors.

"Kelly, wait!" Damian yelled at me. He caught me as I stomped towards the front door and pulled me back towards him.

"I was joking, okay? It was a bad joke. I'm sorry."

I was already crying as he held my arms. Damian pulled me closer to his chest.

"I did go to New York to find out what was going on and I spent time there trying to fix this mess. Once I had a solution, I immediately started to come back here to see you. I was more than halfway here when Shannon called me and said you were on your way to New York to see me. She told me how she and James came to you, and how James was taking you to the city. I didn't see any sense in trying to get back there to find you, so I came here. I was hoping to finish making breakfast and then bring it to you at your house, but you beat me to the punch."

"And what's your solution?" I asked him.

"It was all pretty easy actually. I should have been able to come up with this before. Since my company owns the property now, we don't have to do anything with it we don't want to. So, I am going to rescind all the eviction letters. Anyone that wants to take the buyout will get their money, no questions asked. Anyone that wants to stay can stay. If we have some space to use, I would like to build a small satellite office down here, but if it isn't on the boardwalk, I'm okay with that. I'm sure we can find another space to use. So, the bakery is still yours, for as long as you want it, and at a better rent than what you were paying. That previous company was ripping you off."

I was happy over what I was hearing, but we still had things to say and work out.

"Shannon and James did talk to me," I said through my tears. "I'm sorry about the misunderstanding with that, and with all that happened with the letter, the buyout, and everything. I know I jumped to conclusions about you, Damian. I let my judgment get clouded by expectations and what I had seen in the past. But even with all that, I don't know... I don't know if this will work."

"Why not, Kelly? Look, in case you haven't noticed, I am crazy about you, and I thought you felt the same way about me. I've never fallen for anyone this fast in my life, and now that I have, I don't want to lose you, especially over silly misunderstandings or because you think we're so different that it will never work out. I'm just a guy who is falling in love with someone, plain and simple."

My heart swelled when I heard him say he loved me, and I embraced Damian tightly. I turned to look up at him, and he gently moved some of the damp strands of hair out of my face with his fingers. He took my face into his hands and placed a slow kiss on my lips. The kiss lingered, and I never wanted it to end. When we finally parted, Damian began to wipe my face lightly with his fingers.

"Sorry, I got some flour on your cheeks," he said with a smile.

"You were working in the kitchen without wearing any gloves?" I said in mock anger.

"I guess I was. I didn't really think about it at the time. Honestly, I didn't think anyone would see me here. Does it matter?"

"Does it matter?!" "You have a lot to learn about working in food preparation."

I took Damian by the hand and led him back into the kitchen. As we got through the doors, he pulled me back towards him, kissed me, and lifted me off the floor. I wrapped my feet around him as he pressed me against one of the refrigerators, kissing me deeply.

"Damian," said breathlessly, "My family is going to come walking through that door in an hour or so. We don't have time for this here."

Damian put me back down.

"You're right," he said to me. He led me back out to the storefront, turning off the lights as we moved.

"Let's lock up and go back to my house. If we hurry, we can make good use of that hour."

We walked outside, locked the front door, grasped hands, and ran down the slippery boardwalk, laughing all the way towards Damian's home.

Epilogue

Damian

Four months had passed since that August where Kelly and I first met, first dated, first made love, first fought, and first made up. It was a whirlwind as we found a compromise of time to get to know each other better and time to work with our hectic schedules. I found myself spending more and more time in Delaware as the weeks wore on, from the end of summer and beyond. I hated the days where I had to come back to New York for office work or meetings and had set up an office in my house down here while plans were put in place to build the satellite office for the business in Bethany.

In the end, I decided the boardwalk was no place for an office like what we wanted. I wanted the boardwalk to remain a place of fun, of tourism, and a place for the town to be proud of so that they could grow and thrive. My money could be more usefully spent opening a larger office somewhere else in town where we could have proper facilities, a laboratory and anything else that we might need to keep things moving forward. The town was more than happy to oblige our wishes since we would be bringing tax dollars and employment to the area that went beyond tourism, and the ground was broken in September for our new office, with the hopes of being ready for summer of the following year.

With all that in mind, that didn't mean I wasn't up for making some changes on the new property I owned. Since some of the businesses had opted for the cash buyout, there was no suddenly more room around the bakery. This empty space gave Kelly the perfect opportunity to expand the bakery and grow it into something she had always wanted. We set to work right away on demolition and building so she could have the bigger kitchen, larger seating area, and a place to showcase her skills for bread, cakes, and cake decorating. The changes allowed her to make a bigger name for herself so that the bakery would be a destination point for tourists, locals, and a wider circle out.

The growth also let her do more things for her family. Kelly was able to give Jodie more responsibility with the business, letting her take a larger managerial role in running things and overseeing the additional staff they were able to bring on now. Kelly's Mom was able to cut back and work a lot less if she wanted to, which she rarely did, and while she was still a regular face in the bakery, she didn't have to put in the hours and effort.

So here we were, with December rolling around, most of the tourism going quiet and the holidays coming around the corner fast. I spent a lot of time rattling around in my big house by myself since Shannon and James had gotten a place of their own at the beach instead of staying with me. They had more privacy, but they also took advantage of using the indoor pool and the gym at my house whenever they wanted. Of course, Kelly was here more and more also, to the point where Alice spent more time at my house as my guard dog and companion while I worked.

When Christmas Eve came around, I had walked down to the bakery as it got near to closing time, something that had become a ritual of mine so that I could walk back with Kelly. The bakery had been very busy in the weeks leading up to Christmas, with cookie and cake orders coming in at a rapid pace so that Kelly and everyone at the bakery were working long days. Even when I got to the bakery on Christmas Eve, there were still people picking up items and getting last-minute desserts and snacks.

I walked by the expanded area of the bakery, where there was now a large display window so those strolling by could watch as Kelly decorated a cake or others made cookies or pastries. Kelly spied me walking out of the corner of her eye and gave me a wink.

I entered and said some hellos to a few locals that I recognized. I had become much more a part of the community than I ever thought I could or ever had when I was in New York all the time, and I was much happier for it. I saw Alex behind the counter as I came in.

"Hi, Damian," she said to me as she wiped the counter down.

"Do you have my jelly donut, Alex?" I asked her. She quickly tossed me a white bakery bag that housed my donut, Something I made sure to get regularly when I stopped in.

"Are you all set for the party tonight?" I asked her.

"You bet," she said with a smile. "It's okay if I bring Tyler, right?"

"Sure, but I thought you were dating someone else," I said quizzically.

"Oh, you mean Brad. No, Brad's gone. Tyler is back in the picture now."

"Okay, sure, bring him along."

"Alex, get back to cleaning, or we are never getting out of here tonight!" Jodie yelled as she peeked out the kitchen door. "Hi, Damian. See you tonight," she said to me with a smile.

I looked over to where Kelly had been decorating a cake, but she wasn't there. Instead, she was standing next to me now, putting her arm around me.

"All set?" I said to her.

"I think that was the last cake," she said to me. "It will be nice to have a couple of days off now. I'll see you at the house later Jodie," she yelled as we walked towards the door.

Kelly and I strolled the boardwalk back towards the house. There was a chill in the air, and the clouds were overcast and looked almost like they might bring some snow down.

"Wouldn't it be great to have some snow tonight?" Kelly said to me. "I can't remember the last time we had snow for Christmas down here."

Kelly put her arm through mine and snuggled up close to me as we walked the rest of the way to the house.

The house was decorated to the hilt for the holidays, with a beautiful live tree as the centerpiece upstairs. We had made some catering arrangements for the party we were having, just with Kelly's family, and with Shannon and James. Everyone arrived at around seven, and we ate, drank, laughed, listened to music and had a great time. We shared presents with everyone, including a gift from Kelly and me to the whole family for a cruise we would take next year.

By the time everyone had gone home, it was close to midnight. The last of the catering and cleaning crew had just left, and I saw Kelly curled up on the couch, the fireplace going with a nice fire, the tree lit against the backdrop of the night sky. I sat down on the couch next to her, pulling her close to me.

"Did you have fun tonight?" I asked her.

"It was wonderful," she said kissing me. "I think it was the best family Christmas party yet. Thank you. I hope you had a good time."

"Are you kidding? I never got to have a holiday experience like this. Sure, it was fun with my brothers, but this just felt different. You could see that everyone was relaxed, having a good time, enjoying each other's company. It sounds silly, but there was a lot of love in the house tonight, and that's something I have been missing out on for a long time that you brought into my life."

Kelly leaned in and kissed me, and the snuggled close to me again, laying against my chest. I heard the clock on the mantle start to strike, and I sat up.

"It's midnight," I said to her softly.

"Does that mean you want to go to bed?" she said with a frisky tone.

"Well, when you say it like that, yes. But what I really meant is that it's Christmas. Merry Christmas, Kelly."

Kelly smiled back at me. "Merry Christmas, Damian. Does that mean I can give you a present?" she asked.

"I thought my present was the going to bed part," I told her as I reached for the buttons on the front of her dress.

"Hmmm, not quite yet, mister," she told me and got up off the couch. She went over to the tree and plucked one of the presents from underneath.

"Here," she said handing me the small rectangular box.

"Thanks," I said to her, lightly shaking the box.

"Let me tell you, it is not easy to shop for the billionaire who has everything," Kelly said to me.

I gently opened the paper and took the lid off the box. Inside was a multitool, something I had my eye on for a while.

"Hey, this is great," I said joyfully.

"James said you are always eyeing the one he has, so he helped me get one for you. I hope you like it."

"I love it, thank you," I told her, kissing her.

I sat back on the couch and reached to the table behind it, taking my glass of wine and sipping it.

"Well?" Kelly said to me.

"Well, what?" I asked innocently.

"Do I get to open a present too?" she said impatiently.

"I guess so," I said to her. "I think there's one in a green box under the tree for you," I said pointing.

Kelly bounded over to the tree, searching under it to find a green box. She looked for a few moments before stating:

"Damian, there's no green box under here."

When she turned around, I was right behind her, down on one knee, holding the green ring box in my hand.

"I know," I said to her. "I have it here."

Tears came to her eyes as her hands went to cover the gasp that escaped from her mouth.

"Kelly, I never imagined that four months ago my life would change for the better as much as it has, and it's all because of you. I want this feeling to last for the rest of my life. I love you. Will you marry me?"

I flipped open the ring box to reveal the diamond ring for her and held it out to her. Kelly's hands trembled as she took the box from me and held it. She looked down at me and then knelt next to me on the floor.

"I love you too, Damian, and yes, I will marry you."

I took the ring out of the box and slid it onto her finger. She hugged me tightly and kissed me over and over, with the last kiss being a long one.

"How long have you been planning this?" she asked through her tears.

"In my head? For a few months. I knew a long time ago I wanted to marry you. The actual planning? About a month. I asked your mother for permission first, and then it took some covert operations involving your sisters and Shannon to get your ring size, but I did pick out the ring myself. I will take credit for that," I said proudly.

"You did a fine job, Mr. Woods. It's beautiful," she said as she looked at the ring.

"Not nearly as beautiful as you, future Mrs. Woods," I told her. I stood up and then held out my hand to help her up and then led her off to the bedroom. Alice was already sound asleep in the comfy bed we had purchased for her as a Christmas gift. We stood next to the bed and kissed and then I heard Kelly gasp.

"What?" I asked her.

"I think it's snowing out," she said to me.

Kelly took me by the hand and opened the door leading out to the deck. We stood outside, just as we had those four months ago when she first came into my life and my home. The snow fell lightly and gently and looked amazing as we gazed out to the beach and the water.

"I don't think this day can get more perfect," I said to Kelly, with my arm around her.

"I think it can," she said slyly, as she backed away from me, going into the bedroom as she slowly undid the buttons on her dress.

I closed the door behind me and turned the lights in the room off before joining Kelly on the bed, leaving the only light coming in from outside so we could still see the snow falling outside.